THE TINY FIREBALL

SAMEER KOCHURE

Copyright © 2022 by Sameer Kochure.

All rights reserved. No part of this publication may be reproduced, distributed or transmitted in any form or by any means, including photocopying, recording, or other electronic or mechanical methods, without the prior written permission of the publisher, except in the case of brief quotations embodied in critical reviews and certain other noncommercial uses permitted by copyright law. For permission requests, write to the publisher at the address below.

Written and Published by Sameer Kochure.

Publisher Address:

B19, Sangam CHS, Sai Baba Road,

Off SV Road, Santacruz West,

Mumbai - 54, India.

Printed by Lightning Source UK Ltd., Milton Keynes, UK.

Publisher's Note: This is a work of fiction. Names, characters, places, concepts, and ideas are a product of the author's imagination. Locales and public names are sometimes used for atmospheric purposes. Any resemblance to actual people, living or dead, or to businesses, companies, events, institutions, or locales is completely coincidental.

Published by Sameer Kochure.

ISBN 9789357371247

The Tiny Fireball by Sameer Kochure — First Edition | Paperback

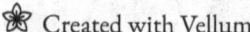 Created with Vellum

About the Book

The tiny Fireball was like a mother's embrace, a kiss from a soulmate, the hug of a daughter never born, a dream pined for an eternity, finally realised.

Welcome to a magical, star-hopping adventure of a lifetime.

In the middle of a desolate, liquid landscape, where food, water and hope runs low, an unusual friendship forms.

One can't see the light, the other is full of sunshine.

Travel with these strange new friends to strange new worlds, in an adventure shrouded in darkness and dipped in honey.

There's magic, there's mysticism, and then, there's the tiny Fireball. Before you know it, she will charm her way into your heart.

ABOUT THE BOOK

You'll never see her coming, and you'll never want her to leave.

∽

Fans of Neil Gaiman's 'The Ocean at the End of the Lane', Antoine de Saint-Exupéry's 'The Little Prince' and Yann Martel's 'Life of Pi' will love Amazon #1 Bestselling Author Sameer Kochure's 'The tiny Fireball'.

Fans of Paulo Coelho's 'The Alchemist', Richard Bach's 'Illusions' and Herman Hesse's 'Siddhartha' will also find comfort and joy in this timeless tale.

So, grab the tiny Fireball's hand and take off on a star-hopping journey of a lifetime.

∽

About the Author:

The tiny Fireball is a magical realism novel with shades of sci-fi fantasy. Written by Sameer Kochure - Amazon #1 Bestselling Author of the beloved book series **'A Young Boy and His Best Friend, the Universe'** and **'Made of Flowers and Steel'** - a poetry collection that celebrates the raw grit behind the beauty that is a woman.

To know more about the the author visit his official website **www.ChannelingHigherWisdom.com**

Contents

1. Ginormous — 13
2. Theories and Speculations — 15
   Distress Signals — 19
3. The Morning of — 20
4. The Appearance — 24
5. Unopened — 30
6. The Night of the Bombing — 33
7. Bottoms Up Schools — 38
8. Saints and Silence — 40
9. Travelling Stars — 44
10. Galactic Adventurers — 47
11. Home Star — 50
12. First Sight — 52
13. Ms. Birdbrain — 56
14. Balloons and Hammocks — 58
15. Illusions — 63
16. A Friend — 66
17. Written in the Ethers — 69
18. Fire on Fire — 72
19. Noble Star #1 — 74
20. Noble Star #2 — 80
21. Noble Star #3 — 86
22. Noble Star #4 — 94
23. Disappearing Act — 97
24. Noble Star #5 — 100
25. Noble Star #6 — 104
26. Outlandish — 110

27. Noble Star #7	112
28. A Logistical Problem	120
29. My Miracle Maker	123
30. Destination Sol	125
31. An Extraordinary Decision	128
32. The Party of the Millennium	130
33. The Second Extraordinary Decision	134
34. The Desire to Live	138
35. An Unexpected Visitor	142
36. The Calm	148
37. The Storm	152
38. A Priceless Gift	159
39. Moth?	163
Epilogue	166
Made of Flowers and Steel	173
More Goodies For You	175
Acknowledgments	177
Also by Sameer Kochure	178
An Appeal	179
A Gift With Your Name On It	180
About the Author	182
Buy or Borrow	184
Gratitude	185

To my Mom, my Aai,
Sunanda Pramod Kochure,
the light of my life,
my first sunrise.

The best way to know God is to love many things.

— VINCENT VAN GOGH

Learn how to see. Realise that everything is connected to everything else.

— LEONARDO DA VINCI

...(sweet smiles)...

— THE TINY FIREBALL

Ginormous

Fireball was tiny, like a little spark riding high above the fire, but she glowed bright, like a billion suns.

When I remarked on her small stature, she said, "Appearance is an illusion. Want me to be ginormous?" and she flew in real close to my eye, almost touching my corneas. I was afraid I'll get burnt by the scorching heat of the suns she carried, but instead, I was enveloped in peace.

As she filled my vision, while no physical contact was made, I felt the warmth of her embrace. As if her love, her light, reached parts of me that had lain forgotten, dusty and undisturbed, under the weights this world had placed upon my soul.

Up close, she looked like a newborn child, like the most beautiful thing I had ever seen. I found myself thinking, if love were to clothe itself in a physical form, this is what it would look like.

As if hearing my thoughts, she burst out laughing.

Oh, how she laughed.

If you would have asked me in that moment what was the sweetest sound in the universe, I had the answer ready for you.

I don't think science, with all its genius and modern technology, would have been successful in precisely measuring her size and scale, tiny as she was, but over the short period of time I spent with her, I grew in agreement with one of the first things she told me.

Appearance is an illusion.

The smallest creation of this universe can fill the universe in our heart.

When viewed with the inner heart, the smallest and the seemingly insignificant turns to timeless and profound.

Theories and Speculations

If you were going to be shipwrecked and you had the choice to be shipwrecked at any time of your choosing, past or present, you would be wise to choose to be shipwrecked today. International shipping routes, commercial and cargo planes, private jets, satellites covering every corner of Earth, government and corporation run space shuttles and a record number of astronauts looking down at Earth from space; means your chances of being rescued are the highest than they have ever been in history.

Rescue is not certain of course. If you are not found within the first three days, your chances of being rescued are as good as winning a lottery. Seven days stranded at sea, and your chances are now similar to winning one of those mega draws when there's no big winner for months, with a prize figure ending in a ridiculous number of zeroes.

I won one of those lotteries once.

Not the money kind, the rescue kind. When I was 9, my parents packed our belongings in aluminium trunks, boarded a steamer with dreams of a richer future in a faraway land, a land they never got to see, for our third night at sea was the last one at sea for our steamer and the last one on Earth for my parents.

136 survivors were rescued the next day by a holiday cruise, 42 were feared lost forever. That number was later corrected to 41.

After 109 days.

The day I won my lottery.

Newspapers ran big photos of my skinny torso and hollow face with headlines like 'Born to Survive', 'The Brave Sailor', 'A Miracle', or something similar. Small passport photos of my parents from the immigration office made an occasional appearance. They were far from flattering, but I treasured them. They were the only records I had of them, all our pretty pictures were safely locked in aluminium trunks stowed away at the bottom of the ocean.

The shipping company magnanimously offered to take care of my education, my boarding, and offered a small stipend till I turned 25 or found myself a job. They even offered me a lifetime of free travel on any of their holiday cruises. This last point was highly debated in the newspapers too. Some found it to be a cruel joke played on a traumatised shipwreck survivor, others argued that my chances of being in another shipwreck in my lifetime were practically zero. They had charts and statistics to back their theories.

Those theories convinced me easily, I had nothing left to lose. I have taken 32 cruises since. All of them were wonderful.

I like the cruise crowd. Holiday goers, retirees, seminar attendees, ill-behaved children, entertainers, staff numbering in hundreds, everyone friendly and jovial, knowing fully well that once we drop the final anchor, we are never going to see each other again.

That's my kind of crowd.

On hearing this, the tiny Fireball said, "So, you move through crowds without making a single lasting connection. You can't lose a friend you never made, right?"

"Right!" I blurted out, then stared at her as she smiled one of her serene smiles.

People smile with judgement, avarice, scorn, all kinds of emotions in their eyes. The tiny Fireball only had love, innocence and a deep understanding behind all her smiles.

It's such a rare treasure, to find someone you can just talk to.

Maybe, subconsciously, I have been looking to reclaim from the sea the connections I lost at sea - that's a theory my shrink, Dr Wadeson, talks about often. This mind doctor is paid for by the shipping liner as well. I don't mind seeing him twice a month, it gives me something to do. How much progress we are making is suspect, but I like the walk to his office that takes me across a bakery which always has bread toasting in the oven, and I am sure the shipping liner has carpeted Dr Wadeson's office a few times over.

I have learnt to take his, and all expert theories in general, as nothing more than wild speculations. Remember those newspaper experts who theorised my odds of getting in another shipwreck in my lifetime were practically zero?

My 33rd voyage proved them wrong and landed me on this little life raft, all alone, until the tiny Fireball showed up.

Distress Signals

There are 16 distress signals that immediately register a new case with the coastguard. The coastguard then launch an investigation, and if all signs point to a missing vessel or people at sea, a Search and Rescue (SAR) operation is initiated.

It helps to know what these distress signals are, should you ever need to send one in an emergency.

In case you are wondering, like the tiny Fireball did when I told her about these signals — no, a message in a bottle is not one of them.

The Morning of

D id the tiny Fireball teleport, crash-land on an UFO, arrive on an asteroid, I couldn't tell you for sure. I can only narrate the facts as they unfolded.

I woke up and there she was.

It was supposed to be an extraordinary day, for I had made an extraordinary decision the night before. A decision that would define my life. Whenever they spoke of me, they would wonder how I, the Miracle boy, made this extraordinary choice.

Like all unexplained phenomena, for a brief moment in time, until the topic faded and died a natural death, I would be a legend.

I had laughed out loud when that thought had occurred to me.

We like to give our lives so much importance; we like

to think our every choice is debated upon, our every decision carefully analysed, we base our moves upon what would people think, how will this land. Such a tiresome job, this perception management business.

The reality is, no one cares.

Sure, people like to talk about others, because it distracts them from the mess their own lives are at the moment, but no one truly cares.

So, why do we care so much about them?

I had stopped caring about what *other* people, the people that don't matter, think of me a long time ago. But I had a hard time letting go of what people I care about think of me. Before I could master that lesson, people I care for had let go of me. Either they let go of me, or this life, this sea, had washed them away into oblivion.

I am sorry to bore you with my brooding, I just want to paint an honest picture of the affairs as they stood that morning when, suddenly, I found myself face to face with the tiny Fireball.

I was instantly amused.

She looked like a figment of my imagination. The isolation, the sea can do that to you sometimes, but those illusions don't last.

She was real alright, as real as me narrating this tale and as real as you listening to it. I will still not force my opinion upon you, I will let you decide for yourself the veracity of this tale.

Why should you care about what I believe.

To help you see her like I did, I will now attempt to undertake a nearly impossible task of describing her physical appearance to you.

The Appearance

Fireball was literally a spark, a starlight, a speck of twinkling light.

Sometimes she appeared like a star, the kind kindergarten kids draw in their books, or get it drawn on their arms by their teachers for being good.

Other times, the tiny Fireball appeared so bright, that all edges and semblance of any physical shape were blurred out by her luminosity. Then, she was like a star shining bright in the sky, physical and visible, but indiscernible to the eye.

Did I imagine her?

Make her up in my mind out of starvation, delusion, or as a way to distract myself from my isolation? I leave you to draw your own conclusions. I will say this though, when you look up at the night sky and describe the stars shining overhead to someone who looks up at the cloudy sky above their heads, do the stars you describe not exist?

The tiny Fireball was made of magic and mysticism. We grownups, mature human beings, have such a tough time accepting the concept of magic, while we live and breathe in it every moment.

Look at a blade of grass. You can put it under a microscope, make a cross section, reduce it to its precise chemical and physical compounds, and measure them in a lab.

Then you can gather those individual elements, put them together in a Petri dish and try to turn them into a blade of grass. Technically, if all the elements are present in the precise quantity, grass should grow again, right?

Except all the elements are not present in that Petri dish.

The magic, the intelligence, the universal love, call it what you will, is missing. That's why there are so many mums and dads waiting to be mums and dads.

There is a certain magic that works behind the curtains of time and space that makes the world go round, grows a blade of grass, and is the cause of you and me.

That same magic manifests creatures of wonder like the tiny Fireball.

All our skepticism doesn't bother it, it just goes on

working its magic. It endows all its creations with a specific purpose.

Perhaps that intelligence, that magic, manifested the tiny Fireball, just so that, one fine day, you could meet her and learn from her how to live and how to love.

And how to sacrifice our *self* for our true love.

While I have done my best to describe the tiny Fireball, I think I have done a pretty poor job of it. So, I will just draw you a picture of what she looked like.

At times, she looked like this:

THE TINY FIREBALL

Sometimes, she appeared small:

Other times, she looked like this:

Sometimes, a bit larger, like this:

I am pretty sure I have failed miserably in capturing her likeness, but I can tell you this. If she were to see these drawings I made of her, we would be treated to another one of her adorable laughs, and the world would be a happier place for it.

SOS signal in Morse Code: Three dots, three dashes, three dots.

Unopened

Water has a beautiful softness to it. I could look at it for hours. I *have* looked at it for hours, even days, perhaps weeks.

One of the things you lose at the sea is your sense of time. When the sun rises, the day begins, when it is overheard and the heat is unbearable, it's midday, when darkness falls, you call it a night.

Except, sometimes, darkness falls right in the middle of a warm, sunny day. The light is hard to find.

So, I try to keep my mind occupied. I have developed a thing, and you are welcome to try it. I call it the water meditation. This is how it works.

You observe water.

That's it, one single step. Just observe water. It can teach you things, for water is wise.

You observe it, you take it all in. The way it flows, the

way it moves, the ripples it makes, the diamonds that dance on its surface. The pearls made by the sun, the moon, the stars, or later, from the tiny Fireball.

You let it flow.

This is the important thing it teaches you. You can row your boat, adjust your sails, navigate with the wind, but you can never direct its flow. It flows as it wants to, like the universe spins the way it wants to. I can put my hands up and cry, I can scream and shout, I can fight and insist, but I can't change the direction of its flow, nor can I control its speed.

I have to let it flow the way it will.

I have to respect it.

Only when I accept it, can I work with it. Water, like everything in nature, is always pointing the way. You just have to learn to see it.

When my second cruise was going down, there was a sense of mild acceptance in my mind. I didn't have any fight left in me. I was ready. I would finally get to open those steel trunks with my toys that were hiding all the colours from my world.

Thoughts of such nature were playing beneath the surface, when something big snapped from my sinking ship, and I flew through the open space for a moment and crashed into the water. I must have made a splash, but it felt more like a splatter in my head. It felt like running into a brick wall head first. I felt every bone in my body rattle. The icy waves shot electric currents through my body. My breath escaped me.

In the next instant, I was struggling to break the surface, my lungs were burning even as I was gulping down salt water by the mouthfuls. I was fighting for the very life I had resigned a few seconds ago.

That, my friend, is the water's great, quiet wisdom in action.

In that instant, the water shook me, woke me, told me to fight on. Fight I did. I held on, and I am glad I did. How else would you have met the tiny Fireball, if I wasn't around to meet her?

Sometimes, you have to leave those steel trunks unopened.

The Night of the Bombing

I remember that night well, the night when, perhaps for the only time, I saw the tiny Fireball being truly afraid.

I had somehow managed to fall asleep. The sea had rumbled through my stomach, keeping me up the last few nights, but this night had come with a reprieve. The breeze was getting cooler all evening, and the starless night lulled me into much needed oblivion.

It couldn't have been much later, when the tiny Fireball shook me awake.

"Something is happening," she said, panic in her voice.

"What do you mean?" I asked, suddenly wide awake.

"I think we are being bombed," Fireball said looking at the dark sky.

I looked at the sky and couldn't see a thing. If there was someone out there, that was a good sign. We were found and could be saved after all.

Except, I couldn't see nor hear anyone. I was straining, of course, a desperate being straining long and hard for a glimmer of hope. But all I could see was the dark sky.

I said, "Maybe you had a bad dream."

She violently shook her head, white in the face.

Then I felt the first bomb land right in the space between us.

It didn't explode, it splashed.

I wanted to laugh, but in the same breath, as the small raindrop crashed on the raft and sprayed even smaller drops on my feet, I saw a droplet brush against the tiny Fireball. It sizzled and put out a small part of her, as she winced in agony.

I shuddered. It was not going to be just a bombing.

It was going to be an invasion.

I scrambled, looked everywhere on the raft. Something, surely there must be something that could keep us both safe.

I shouted at her to move closer to me, shielding her with my body as I continued searching through our meagre worldly possessions.

Suddenly the night sky was lit up like a Hydrogen bomb had gone off somewhere in the heavens, ready to breathe hellfire upon us.

I was running out of time. I had to think fast.

I grabbed the peanut butter jar, the one holding the last of our drinking water, and without hesitation, I emptied it into the sea.

THE TINY FIREBALL

"Here, quick," I commanded.

She quickly jumped into the jar, I fastened the lid, and clutched it close to my heart.

That very instant, the bombing began.

I shudder to think what would have happened if I was but a moment late.

Giant raindrops crashed on to our little raft. If I was alone, I would have bathed and rejoiced. Drank my fill and stored as much fresh water as I could. But I had the tiny Fireball with me.

That night, as I was getting drenched, for the first time, I understood the bigger danger we were in. We were floating in the middle of nowhere on a battered raft.

The tiny Fireball was literally a spark, surrounded by the high seas.

A lazy wave, an innocent gust of wind, a well-intentioned backsplash could extinguish and wipe her out forever.

Scared I won't be able to keep her safe, I found myself shouting at her, "Of all the places you could have landed on this planet, why did you choose my tiny raft?"

She didn't say a word.

She just slid to the bottom of the peanut butter jar, pulled her knees close and buried her head in them.

The rain and the thunder were deafening. But through it all, I heard her sobbing.

That sound still keeps me up at night.

She was my friend. I would have given my life to save

her that night. So why was I being so mean to her?

Why are we sometimes so harsh to the ones we so adore?

Sound Fog Horn. Continue sounding
the Fog Horn to attract attention.

Bottoms Up Schools

All my memories of the tiny Fireball are not tied to the things or events that happened to us at the sea, but to the feelings she arose in me. The strongest memories belong to the times when she made me feel absolutely stupid, without any malice, mind you. I don't think she was capable of feeling malice towards anyone. It was as if that emotion could not have been part of her, or if it was, and I lean towards the possibility that it once was, then she had long ago learnt how to let go of it for good.

The one time she found me particularly stupid was when she found out about the schooling system on Earth. She wasn't surprised to know that children and grownups came together at schools for the purpose of a higher education. 'That is how it should be,' she said sagely, but she was horrified on hearing the roles they play at school. She found it to be absolutely bonkers.

"Kids go to schools to learn from adults??" she said and broke into one of her laughs.

"Why, you have schools that are bottoms up. What a funny thought!"

She must have laughed for a full seven minutes while I looked lost. When she finally came to, I asked, "what's so funny?"

She said, "Don't you see? Your schools are upside down. Grownups teach kids! How silly, don't you realise grownups have so much more to learn from children? That's how schools everywhere I have travelled to in the universe work. Who came up with this idea? I bet it was a grownup."

After the moment had faded, in a more sombre voice she said, "that explains it though..."

"Explains what?" I asked.

"It explains why people on this planet seem to struggle with love so much... you are not learning about it from the ones who can teach it to you best."

I stared at her for a long time, while she sat there, beaming one of her kindest smiles at me.

By then I had already started loving the tiny Fireball like she was my child, but that was the moment when, at a deeper level as yet unknown to me, I accepted her as my teacher.

Saints and Silence

The tiny Fireball was like a mother's embrace, a kiss from a soulmate, the hug of a daughter never born, a dream pined for an eternity, finally realised.

How did she end up on this little life raft with me?

I thought about it often, even asked her for details more than once, but it was not possible to direct the flow of conversation with her.

She spoke about the things she wanted to talk about, and then she was simply silent. Not cutting you off, avoiding you or giving you the cold treatment.

She preferred sharing, and enjoying a divine silence.

When I remarked about her lack of speech, she said, "If we are talking all the time, we might miss out on what the universe is trying to tell us."

I asked, "what is the universe trying to tell us right now?"

"Find out for yourself... be quiet and listen."
"But how...?"
"Shhh..." she shushed me, smiling.

I smiled, it was hard not to smile with her, even when she was shushing you.

I tried. I didn't hear a thing. Well, either she was cuckoo, or she was clearly not from around here.

I must add a note here about her silence though. Even if she wasn't speaking, the tiny Fireball was always present with you a hundred per cent.

It was like, if she was dancing, she was dancing totally. Not thinking about how she looked, not wishing for her favourite song, not worried about her uncomfortable shoes, neither hoping for a better dance partner, nor looking for someone to lead.

In that moment, she was simply dancing - with the totality of her being.

In that moment, she was doing nothing else, she became the song, she became the dance.

Once an old and a wise soul had given me a definition of a saint which I have never forgotten, probably because it was not a religious, but a practical, relatable definition. He told me that a saint is someone who talks when he talks, eats when he eats, sleeps when he sleeps.

Simple.

Profound if you think about it.

Of course, I never saw the tiny Fireball put on her comfy shoes, throw back her hair and dance like we were on a night-out, but that's how I imagine she would have done it, like she did everything else.

She brought her complete presence to the present moment.

I gave the example of dancing just to illustrate a point. Besides, it is such a lovely thought to imagine her dancing with total surrender, carefree abandon.

I can see her in my mind's eye, grooving and jiving, or whatever you may want to call those crazy moves of hers. Such a joy.

How adorable she looks... by now, you can see her dancing in your mind's eye too, can't you?

SIGNAL 3

Display an Orange distress flag featuring a black square and ball.

Travelling Stars

"Quick, make a wish!" I said.

The tiny Fireball asked, "Why?"

I said, "Look at that, a shooting star."

"Oh, you make a wish at that, that's sweet. But that's not a shooting star, that's a travelling star."

"What do you mean?"

"That's how stars get from one place to the next, they get bored hanging out at one spot too. Sometimes they have work to do in other parts of the galaxy, so they just go there. Sometimes they are looking for answers, so they leave on a quest... how do you think I got here?"

"You got here on a shooting star??"

The tiny Fireball didn't answer, instead got annoyed, like a kindergarten teacher does at her favourite pupil and said, "Do you ever listen to anything I say? Travelling - they are called 'travelling' stars."

THE TINY FIREBALL

"But don't they die after?"

"Nothing in the universe ever dies."

"Oh come on now, don't be silly. That's simply not true."

"Form changes. Just because the star you call a 'shooting' star disappears from your telescope does not mean it has disappeared forever. It went where it had to go, did what it had to do, and then it transformed. Now it exists in a form where your eyes can't see it. Yet."

"Besides," she said, "I would have never set off on my star quest if it involved so many stars dying. I have hopped on seven of them so far, you think I would have travelled with them if it meant seven of them dying forever? Do I seem so cruel to you? Don't you know me at all?"

The tiny Fireball crossed her arms and turned away from me, facing the other side of the desolate ocean. By some unwritten rules, I was not allowed on her side of the raft, till she came to me in her own time.

I was upset that I upset her.

I was also intrigued. Star quest? Hopping ride on stars? What was that all about?

Galactic Adventurers

My hip bones hurt when I sat anywhere on the raft too long. The raft wasn't uncomfortable, the muscle and flesh under my skin had faded. Hunger and thirst were stranded on the raft with us. How could I be angry at them, they were our friends, our constant companions in the big blue nothing.

These thoughts didn't dwell on my mind too long, for I was looking forward to learn about the tiny Fireball's star quest.

"So, tell me, what is it? Are you like a galactic adventurer, travelling through the universe on an epic quest?" I said, laughing.

She looked at me doe-eyed and said, "Aren't we all? Aren't you? Out here, right now, looking for answers in the middle of nowhere..."

"I'm not looking for anything..."

She shrugged and said, "If you say so... anyway, if you want to know about my star quest, you have to ask me the most important question about it first."

"Most important question? I already asked it - what is it?"

"That's not it. The most important question about anything in the universe is *why*? You should consider *why* did I leave my beautiful home and set out on my quest."

"Well, why did you?"

The tiny Fireball looked up at the stars and I followed her gaze. The moon had taken a night off and the sky was lit up with all the stars in the galaxy.

If love had ever shown up in my life, the stars that night would have reminded me of my one true love, the forever kind. But like all good and sensible things, love had kept away from me all my life.

Then I looked at the tiny Fireball and saw something strange sparkle in her eyes. Could it be love, the forever kind?

Then she said, "have I told you about the day a strange moth showed up on my home star?"

Shoot Red Flares to draw attention.

Home Star

The tiny Fireball's home was a star. Just like her, it was aflame. Not burning violently like a volcano erupts, but with a constant, mellow nurturing blaze that plays on our own sun.

Of course, if you try to land on the surface of sun, you would discover the might of it in your brief, final moments as it reduces you to nothingness.

I picked up bits and pieces of information about the tiny Fireball's home from the chance remarks she made in passing. Turns out everything on her home star was ablaze; trees, rivers, sofas, everything. How could one ever be comfortable on a flaming sofa I could never imagine. But then if I hadn't met her, I could have never imagined the tiny Fireball either. So I believed everything she told me, like a child believes all the wonders that grownups tell them about. Logic has no place in magic, and when you are young, untouched by the flawed, perceived realities of the world, everything is magical.

Besides, it made sense.

A flaming being like the tiny Fireball could only be comfortable on a flaming bed. Who wants to keep redecorating again and again because your teak furniture keeps turning to coal.

So, I had accepted the reality that everything on her home star was made of fire, and therefore, I was not surprised to learn that one fine day, out of the blue, a moth was drawn to it.

Even here on planet earth, moths share a strange fatal attraction to fire. Scientists have studied the phenomenon for years, but they are still divided on why the moths do that. All species are geared towards survival. Every action they take is motivated by their inherent need to survive and reproduce. But moths happily fly into flames and give up their lives for no conceivable reason.

As far as I know, throughout history, only one emotion has made us so readily risk our lives without logic or reason — love.

These moths must really love fire.

As the tiny Fireball started telling me about her encounter with the moth, I soon realised that those scientists had failed because they were working with only one half of the story.

First Sight

The tiny Fireball welcomed all odd travellers that visited her home star. I figured they had an open immigration policy.

"You have to visit me soon too!" she said, excited, without really explaining how would I go about booking my trip.

One morning, on her 'home sweet star home' she welcomed a strange creature, the likes of which she had never seen before in the entire universe. This odd creature sauntered in, or rather flew in with the demeanour that seemed to say, *'don't I own this star already?'*

The tiny Fireball was mesmerised by the colourful wings, and said, "Hi, welcome to my home star. I am Fireball... and you are?"

"You *don't* know me? Maybe you are having difficulty recognising me in real life, it happens to us celebrities all the time. Wait let me give you another angle," the stranger said, as she drew her wings in and prepared to land on the couch.

Suddenly, the tiny Fireball screamed, "Stop! I know who you are! You are not welcome here!!"

The stranger stretched out her wings, hovered in the air above the couch and said, "My! You are awfully rude!"

"I'm sorry. That came out wrong. Forgive me..."

"Forgiven. Don't let it happen again."

The stranger was being rude now, but the tiny Fireball let it pass and said, "I've heard stories about you. You are a Moth, aren't you?"

"The one and only. The most beautiful, exquisite and magnificent creature in the entire universe."

The tiny Fireball rolled her eyes, this little Moth was full of herself, whatever else she was, she was not humble.

The tiny Fireball said, "Right. Anyway, my home star is very welcoming of visitors, but I am afraid, we won't be able to extend that courtesy to you today."

"Outrageous! Why not? I demand an answer, and I demand it now!"

"Please, could you not be so dramatic? You can simply ask and I will give you all the answers you need, no need for 'demands' and all."

"I've heard a lot of words, but not my answer yet," said the Moth.

"Uff! Fine, here's your answer," the tiny Fireball was nearing the end of her patience, "You are not welcome here because my home star is not safe for you. Just like me, and everything on it, my home star is made of fire. It will burn you if you step a single foot on it."

"What nonsense! I love fire!" the Moth said and landed on the flaming couch. Immediately her legs started smouldering, she was air bound in the next instant, screaming in agony, "Ouch, ouch, ouch!!"

"See, I told you! Why won't you just listen to me?" said the tiny Fireball and scrambled to grab her first aid kit.

And that was how the tiny Fireball met the Moth.

SIGNAL 5

Leave a sea marker dye trail in the water.

Ms. Birdbrain

The Moth's feet were badly burnt. At least that'll teach her to be more careful in the future, the tiny Fireball thought.

Dressing up her burns, the Moth said, "this is just great... why didn't you stop me from landing on your star, *Firebob*?"

The tiny Fireball put her arms on her hips and frowned, "I tried to stop you! ...and my name is Fireball, you birdbrain."

"Fireball U. Birdbrain - suits you," the Moth threw her head back and laughed.

"Go away!"

"*You* go away. Like seriously, go. All this getting burnt business has been exhausting, I need my beauty sleep now. Shoo..." the Moth dismissed her.

The tiny Fireball said, "Rest? Sleep? Haven't you

learnt your lesson? You can't stay on my home star. It will smoke you up!"

"Well, I can't travel in this condition, now can I?" the Moth said pointing to her bandaged feet.

"And whose fault is that?"

"Come on, don't be too hard on yourself," the Moth said and grinned.

The tiny Fireball fumed at her, while the Moth continued to glide inches above the star that could obliterate her instantly.

The tiny Fireball pleaded, "Why are you doing this?!"

The Moth was silent for a moment.

Then she said, "I... don't... know. Ever since I can remember, I have dreamt of this star. Seen it burning bright, shining like a diamond... I have always wanted to be here... I have heard it calling my name... like it has been calling it all my life... and now that I am here, so near... at my journey's end... and you just want me to *leave*?"

The tiny Fireball felt guilt creep up on her. There was a sincere note in the Moth's voice. She made up her mind - the Moth was staying.

How?

Now that would need some creative thinking.

Balloons and Hammocks

"Wait a second..." I said, "You are saying the Moth simply *appeared* on your home star? It just flew over, across space? Without any rocket, spaceship or anything at all? Forgive me if I find that hard to believe."

The tiny Fireball saw that I was in one of my moods that came about when there were few fish about. She said, "Why are your doubts bigger than your beliefs? You have a problem believing what I tell you, but you have no problem believing you will never sleep on dry land again. Right now, you have no way of knowing if either of these things is 100% true, but you choose to believe the thought that's least helpful for you. That's such a silly way to live, why do that to yourself?"

I stared at her, all my words had flown out of my head into deep space - without any rocket or spaceship.

The tiny Fireball said, "Besides, I never said the Moth

flew in with nothing. She had a backpack, the kind you take with you when you go on a trek or camping."

Of course, I thought silently. A backpack. Everyone knows when you have to make an intergalactic voyage, you have to have a backpack. I asked, "and what was in this backpack?"

"The usual; a towel, a toothbrush, a make-up kit, a few other essentials, and, oh yes, two hammocks."

"Two hammocks? Why?"

"I asked the Moth the same thing, she said, 'you don't

expect me to just sleep anywhere, do you? I must be comfortable.' Then I asked her why *two* hammocks, she said, 'one is a backup; when you are travelling, you never know. I have a backup make-up kit too.'

The tiny Fireball smiled a sweet smile I had never seen on her before and said, "My Moth can be quite vain... always colouring her wings in all shades of pretty."

"What happened then, did you find a safe place for the Moth to get her beauty sleep?"

"I did. Technically not on my home star, but above it. The Moth wouldn't have lasted on the surface of my home star, so I built her a floating villa."

"Wow... how did you do that?"

"I'm calling it a floating villa because that was the only way to get the Moth in it. I convinced her to let me rip her spare hammock and turn it into two hot air balloons. She had the hammock to spare, and I had plenty of fire on my home star to keep the hot air balloons going forever. Then we hung the other hammock at the base of these two hot air balloons. The hammock floated safely above my home star, while staying in orbit thanks to gravity. The Moth could live, rest and sleep in it quite comfortably. A gust of wind may carry her floating villa here or there, but she would always stay in orbit, always close to my home star... always, close to me."

There was that sweet smile again.

Interesting.

SIGNAL 6

Wave arms up and down continuously. (Same position as making snow angels).

Illusions

"The next few days flew by. The Moth had been on my home star for a while, and I found myself spending more and more time with her. How could I not, she's hilarious!"

The tiny Fireball was the most talkative when she was telling me about the Moth.

"I took the Moth along with me on a tour across my home star. She wanted to see every corner of it, so, I showed her everything."

"We would fly together, hovering above surface, at a safe distance for her. The more the Moth saw of my home star, the more she seemed to fall in love with it."

"*How pretty... this is wonderful... Gorgeous... Sooo cute!*" - She would exclaim around every corner. I failed to see what was the big deal. Of course, it was my home star, a place I grew up in, my neighbourhood. I failed to appreciate it when I lived there all my life. Now that I have been away so long, when I see it again, I am sure I will also go,

"How pretty... this is wonderful... Gorgeous... Sooo cute!" - the tiny Fireball imitated her imitation of the Moth and giggled at her silliness. She was so cute when she did that, I could just gobble her up.

"Time and space is an illusion, you know," said the tiny Fireball.

"Appearance, time and space - all illusions. Got it," I said.

"I can never tell if you are being serious," the tiny Fireball smiled, "but they are. If I am thinking of the 'time' I spent with my winged friend, thinking the same thoughts, feeling the same feelings, then I am with her. I am living that same moment with her, right now. To me, it is not 'back then' it is 'right now'."

"Hmmm..." I was kind of following her reasoning, but I was not ready to give in just yet, "How about space? You are here with me and the Moth is back on your home star."

The tiny Fireball smiled and said, "When I am thinking of my friend, thinking of the wonderful memories we shared, missing her, am I not already with her? What 'physical space' can separate us?"

"Where's the distance between our hearts if they are already together?"

Every morning I feel grateful when my feet leave my warm quilt and touch the floor, and by extension, the dry land.

If the tiny Fireball didn't fully convince me back then, she has me convinced today.

It has been a long 'time' since we had that conversation at a place where hope was running on empty. So much 'time' has passed in between. But thinking of that moment, I am transported right back to the edge of that battered raft. I am sitting there with my feet dangling in the sea, having a strange conversation about time, space and other illusions, with my tiny friend, who has my heart, right next to hers. Search as you might, you'll not find any space between them.

So much has happened since, but whenever I think of my sweet little friend, not a single moment has passed where our hearts have been apart.

Time and space, such beautiful illusions.

A Friend

One morning, the tiny Fireball saw the Moth packing her backpack. Surprised, she said, "going somewhere?"

The Moth looked at the tiny Fireball with cloudy eyes and said, "yes. I have admired your home star from far long enough..." the Moth hesitated, and her next words were strained, "It's time for me to go to the surface."

"No, you can't! It will destroy you!"

"Then, let it!" the Moth screamed and threw away her backpack.

The tiny Fireball had never seen the Moth in such agony before. She froze.

A moment passed, and the Moth found her tenderness again. "I'm sorry. Look... you have been kind to me. Taking care of me, showing me your beautiful home from miles away, just to keep me safe. But I have not travelled all this way just to be safe. I have travelled for love."

"I didn't know the name of the feeling before, but I have always felt a great pull towards your home star. It has been beckoning me all my life, drawing me to it forever. Everything I have done in my life has led me to this moment. I thought it was just a whim, but it's beyond that, it's a calling. How and why I do not know. I know I am drawn to your home star with every breath that runs through my veins, it's the dream within all my dreams. So, go I must."

"But it will..."

"...*kill me?* So be it. Every dream demands a payment, and I am prepared to pay it in full."

"There has to be a way for you to go the surface and not be destroyed... there has to be a way!"

"Not that I know of, neither do you. The law of infinity says that everything is possible, so there must be a way to do this safely, we just don't know it."

The tiny Fireball declared, "Then I shall find it."

"How?"

"By going on a star quest to the 8 Nobles."

"No...!" The Moth was shocked. A star quest across 8 Noble Stars was an arduous journey. It involved travelling to the furthest corners of deep space. Rarely would anyone dare taking on such a taxing task.

"You will do no such thing," the Moth said, "I won't let you."

The tiny Fireball was defiant and said, "Try and stop me."

"You can't blackmail me emotionally like this. So many have set off on a star quest to the 8 Nobles, only a few have ever returned. I can't let you risk your life and sit here, do nothing."

"But that's exactly, what you are asking me to do," said the tiny Fireball, smiling.

"That's not fair. Do you want me to give up on my dream? If I don't go after what I have desired so deeply, then my life has no meaning."

The tiny Fireball flew in close to the Moth, looked deep in her eyes and said, "I understand now how much your dream means to you. That's why I want to help you. I will never forgive myself if I didn't do everything in my capacity to help you realise your dream and to be safe."

"The 8 Nobles hold secrets to all life in the universe, one of them will be able to guide us."

"Then let me go, I will travel to the 8 Nobles and ask them..." the Moth pleaded.

The tiny Fireball said gently, "You can't make this journey with your beautiful tiny wings, but I believe, I can. Let me do this for us. I don't want to lose you, I have never had a friend like you before."

The Moth nodded and quickly looked away, trying to hide her tears.

The Moth didn't want to lose the tiny Fireball too. She had never had a friend like her as well.

Written in the Ethers

It was time for the tiny Fireball to leave on her quest. Goodbyes were hard across the universe.

When she could put it off no longer, she came to see her Moth.

She wondered when the Moth became *her* Moth.

They saw each other and the next moment they were in each other's arms, sharing their first hug. No words were spoken, only poems of the heart written in the ethers.

The tiny Fireball saw small sparks start to sizzle over the Moth's wings and said, "Stop! This is hurting you!!"

"Just a moment longer..." the Moth said. "Even this pain will become a memory of us."

The tiny Fireball didn't quite understand, but she didn't let go either.

Love was the same across the universe.

SIGNAL
7

Fire gunshots at 1 minute intervals.
Three at a time.

Fire on Fire

The tiny Fireball called it star-hopping and made it sound easy, like the game we used to play with our friends when we were young and the world was sunny.

As I soon discovered, the reality was different.

Star-hopping was like a trial by fire.

Shooting stars look pretty in the night sky - when we are looking at them from a safe distance. But they are literally on fire.

A star made of fire is set on fire as it hurtles through space.

I asked the tiny Fireball, "What do all these celestial travellers use for fuel?"

The tiny Fireball said, "You can only travel light through the universe. Anything that is heavy, impure and gross needs to be burnt away and is therefore usually used as a fuel. To travel far and wide, to go anywhere worthwhile in this universe, you have to turn into simple and light."

I nodded my head, put on my stoic face and said, "I get that. I am on this raft with barely any possessions, and meeting you, talking to you makes me feel simple and light as well."

The tiny Fireball smiled.

My stomach grumbled, our fishing line had been limp for the last few days, we had nothing left to use as bait.

I smiled back and said, "Of course, I wish we hadn't met under such pitiful and painful circumstances."

The tiny Fireball said, "Pain lights the fire. Purges everything gross and impure. The fire lights the way."

I was about to ask her to explain, when I felt something small and weak tug on the fishing line.

Judging by its pull on the string, it was far from heavy and almost certainly gross.

However, in that moment it felt nothing short of a royal feast.

Noble Star #1

To understand a thing, is to see it clearly. To see, for the first time, the truth of it.

— FROM THE TRAVEL DIARIES OF THE
TINY FIREBALL.

The tiny Fireball felt the most excruciating pain all over her body. All parts of her physical self, all her thoughts, all feelings she ever had, every sensation she ever felt; everything was on fire.

Not the usual mellow fire that she simmered with, this was like being shoved into a furnace that could melt a thousand suns.

She wanted to scream, but it seemed like if she did,

even the words that came out of her would instantly be set ablaze. She was dizzy as she was hurtling through space. Just when she thought she could take it no more, the external fire started to fade, became bearable and then disappeared.

She had reached the surface of the first star - Noble #1.

Panting, breathless, she took a few hungry, hurried breaths and felt her heart slowly find its rhythm. Then she took a stock of herself, the next instant she was horrified. It seemed like the very first star-hop had diminished her to half her usual size. Her clothes didn't fit and her shoes were twice as large now. They said the first star-hop is always the hardest. She had made it and reached her first pit-stop.

Before she could panic about her diminished stature, she heard a voice, "Ah welcome dear, long time I had any visitor... My name is Akasha, and what's your name? You must be on your way to the Celestial Kingdom..."

Somewhat regaining her composure, the tiny Fireball looked at the source of voice, it was Noble #1, rocking on a cosy, quilted rocking chair. Instantly she felt her spirit rise.

She smiled at the kind old star, perhaps the oldest star in the universe and said, "Thanks for welcoming me... I am the tiny Fireball. Although I am just here for my friend."

The wise old star smiled and said, "For your friend?? I see."

"Yes, her name is Moth, she is a moth, and she wants to go to the surface of my home star. She will surely get roasted if she does so, moths are not like us, they can't live on stars like we do."

The wise old Noble smiled and stroked his flaming, long white beard and said, "yes, yes... you are right."

"So, I have set off on a star-quest to find a way to save my friend."

The wise old Akasha said, "You already know how to save your friend."

The tiny Fireball looked puzzled.

The wise old Noble smiled and said, "We live our lives

for our own selves. You think you have taken on a mission for your friend? That's not true, you have set off on this quest for - you."

"I don't understand."

"You will by the time your quest is complete. Till then, your quest won't be complete."

"But what about my friend? I only want to save her."

"We all have a special role to play in the Divine plan of Life itself. I have pointed the way. Meditate upon it, go within and you will find all the knowledge and wisdom you need."

"But I will be able to save my friend, yes?" the tiny Fireball insisted.

The wise old Noble, Akasha, looked at her long and hard, then smiled and said, "Your success depends upon your right understanding of everything you experience, encounter and do on your quest."

"Doubting, fearing will only make your journey something it doesn't have to be - painful. Sometimes, you have to give up to get."

"I don't understand what you mean..." the tiny Fireball pleaded.

The Noble Akasha said, "You can't direct the course of love, you can only let it lead you. When you do, it leads you to all the right places."

The tiny Fireball looked up at the wise old Noble and said, "But I have never been in love... how would I know..."

Her words were cut off by the booming laughter of the wise old Noble. Smiling, laughing, he sauntered off, silently wishing success and happy travels to the tiny Fireball, while continuing to laugh like a silly, old, loving grandfather.

The tiny Fireball smiled, the kind old Noble's laugh was infectious. Even if she didn't understand his words, she decided to meditate upon them. She had plenty of time on her journey ahead.

The one lovingly known as 'The Star of Right Understanding' had left her more confused than before.

She shrugged and prepared for her second star-hop.

Radiotelegraph alarm: A series of twelve 4 second dashes, with 1 second intervals, sent in one minute. (Requires technical knowledge and equipment)

Noble Star #2

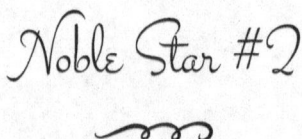

Right Resolution is to make a decision in the light. A decision that sheds darkness, brings simplicity and purpose to your actions.

— FROM THE TRAVEL DIARIES OF THE
TINY FIREBALL.

My tail is on fire? The tiny Fireball thought and laughed, how silly of me, I don't even have a tail!

Then she wondered, how could I feel this intense heat when I am made of fire?

Physics had kicked in, she was being drawn in by the gravity from the second star.

The tossed-in-an-inferno feeling was familiar this time

around, but it wasn't less painful. Everything within her rattled as it was roasted. It's as if I am on a barbecue grill and an invisible hand is rotating the skewer in a hurry to ensure even cooking.

Despite the pain, the tiny Fireball smiled at the thought, she would look like a riot on a skewer.

She knew the pain would get worse for a moment and then it would be alright. Right then, the pain started fading and soon it was gone. She had arrived at the second stop on her star-quest.

She gathered herself and was half surprised to find her clothes too large, and her shoes twice as big, again.

No one told me about this side effect of star-hopping, she thought. Oh well, travel has its surprises.

Then she looked up and was spellbound. This had to be the most beautiful star in the Universe. Everywhere her eye wandered, there were beautiful glittering sculptures made in the finest moonstones.

Stunning works of art depicting the wonders of the universe were strewn all around her. She noticed a planet with 19 moons, a travelling star and a black hole, among others.

All of them were perfect replicas, yet something about them had elevated their forms to divine perfection. The tiny Fireball knew it was impossible, but they appeared more beautiful than reality. She thought, this has to be the work of a master artisan.

Then she saw the artist behind the art.

The tiny Fireball thought the artist looks like a work of art herself.

An angelic face, glowing tresses that seemed to flow to eternity and the kindest, yet most determined eyes she had ever seen. She approached with reverence and said, "Hi... I am the tiny Fireball, and I am on a star-quest to learn how to save my friend."

The Angelic star smiled and said, "You already know how to save your friend..."

The tiny Fireball was about to protest but was interrupted, "...and you are so cute! Would you mind if I make a sculpture of you?"

The tiny Fireball blushed and said, "Me, cute? Why, thanks. Of course, sculpt me all you want. I am sure you can make anything look good."

"We all can," the Angelic Artist said, "if we decide to."

The tiny Fireball said, "That's what you are famous for right? Making right decisions?"

"Right Resolutions is the term I prefer. You should always use the right words, you'll learn more about it on your next hop. There's a hidden power in words. 'Resolution' is unshakable. The world can tilt and lose its axis, but a right resolution once made, holds strong. So many people 'decide', then do otherwise. It takes a powerful spirit to resolve in light, and then make it true. We are all only accountable to our own selves."

The tiny Fireball let it all soak in.

Then she said, "Does 'resolution' help you make these beautiful sculptures too?"

"Absolutely!" the Angelic Artist said, "Want to know how I create my works of art?"

"Yesss please!"

The Angelic Artist walked around her studio, examining raw, uncut moonstones, turning them over and said,

"It's simple. It sometimes starts in my imagination or with a subject, but often it starts with a stone."

She picked one that she liked and scrutinised it from all angles.

"I look at a piece of a moonstone and then I decide, I resolve what I want it to be, what it really wants to be..."

she looked at the stone for a moment and then she closed her fiery eyes.

"Then, I help it become it."

As she said those words, without a single touch, parts of the moonstone crumbled in front of her, dust flew in all directions and when the dusty mist cleared, the tiny Fireball's jaw dropped open as she saw the creation in front of her.

It was a sculpture of a flying moth, with a backpack.

"It's my Moth! The friend I was telling you about!!" The tiny Fireball was jumping around, clapping her hands.

"I know."

"Wow! You made my day!"

The artist smiled and took a bow.

The tiny Fireball said, "Anyway, I need to be on my way soon, I have 6 more stars to get to. Could you please tell me how do I go about saving my friend that you have so beautifully sculpted?"

"I have already shown you all I have to teach you, my love. Meditate upon it on your travels and soon you will understand everything."

The tiny Fireball nodded, "Alright, I will. Thank you for your knowledge and wisdom. And thank you for this wonderful gift," she said, pointing to the sculpture of her friend.

"But you won't be able to carry it dear, it's far too heavy and…"

"I know, it must stay here. It's a good place for it, it

will be surrounded by so much beauty. Even if I can't carry it with me, I still consider it as a gift. Would you do me one more favour please?"

"Tell me..."

"When you make my sculpture, could you please put mine next to this one?"

The Angelic Artist smiled with misty eyes and said, "Of course, my dear."

After what felt like a mother's embrace, the tiny Fireball took off once again.

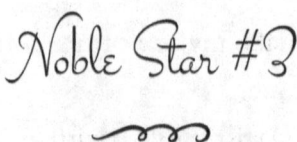

Right speech is expressed in silence. A divine silence undisturbed and unbroken by words.

— FROM THE TRAVEL DIARIES OF THE
TINY FIREBALL.

Back on our little raft in the middle of the Pacific, it was so easy to talk to the tiny Fireball. Listening to the stories of her star-quest, asking her a million questions about it, I realised, she was so easy to talk to because of the way she listened.

We are told good listeners are the ones who listen without judgement, who listen without thinking about what they are going to say next. That's not true, good listeners are the ones who listen with love.

The tiny Fireball said, "Speech is the first gateway through which the inner world meets the outer world."

"What do you mean?"

"Try to understand it without words... in your own silence," she said smiling.

I didn't understand right away, but I turned her words over and over in my head. It was better than thinking about the thirst I felt in my bones.

An eternity later, came the dawn of understanding. It came without words, but I shall try to put it in words for you now.

You have thoughts, feelings, desires, emotions, dreams, ambitions, plans, prayers, wishes, all of them live in your inner world. When you speak about them and express them, they travel on your breath from the inner world to the outer — physical and visible world. You can't see your thoughts, but you can see your words by the vibrations they create on sand or the surface of water. Put you hand in front of your mouth as you speak and you can feel the air being dispersed by your words.

I have therefore decided to call our speech a physical substance, if you disagree, you are welcome to hop onboard my raft and debate it out with me. Just bring some cold water and cookies, will you?

I digress, blame the thirst.

The outer world, our material world is built of physical materials. In the physical world, physical substance creates other physical substance. Soil creates plants, which creates rubber, which is used in the making of life rafts. One cannot exist without the other. Substance is all linked to each other. Therefore our 'physical' words literally build the world we touch and feel around us.

Fix one to fix the other.

All these realisations came to me out of few brief words the tiny Fireball had spoken. If all this comes off too heavy, you must forgive me, I am not her. The tiny Fireball can make it simple and easy. She always said so much with so little. I now realise it was the right use of her substance.

The nature of interdependence also became a little magical for me when I realised my body, the one I so identify easily with, is also made of a certain substance, and if every substance in this world comes from other substance, then I am related to everything that exists, anything and everything that is made of some substance is a cousin of mine, my kin.

And if my speech is creating new substance in this universe, then it is only wise, that I bring out the finest substance through my words, or rest in silence, till I find those finest words.

Having created so many words now, I will rest in the silence for some time and let you continue on with the tiny Fireball's third pit-stop.

THE TINY FIREBALL

The clothes, the shoes, everything was way oversize once again. The tiny Fireball quickly fixed herself up the best she could, and took a look around the newest star on her path.

Something was striking about it, she couldn't quite put her finger on what it was yet. It looked beautiful, serene, glowing with a quiet inner beauty, a sort of halo. She took a few steps over the powdery white surface that had the signature star blaze, mixed with something else. She had arrived tired, it was a red-eye hop, but the minute her feet had made contact, she had felt rested, calmer than she had felt in a long time.

As she sauntered around this serene star, she almost walked into the star keeper, a bald man with midnight coloured skin, draped in luminous robes. He was looking at the tiny Fireball with a deep smile on his face, a smile that may have just appeared for her or may have been there for an eternity.

The tiny Fireball couldn't help but smile back. She smiled and took a bow in front of her new Master. The Master gave a slight nod and looked at her with those kindly eyes.

The tiny Fireball said, "Hello... I am the tiny Fireball. You must be the lord of the third star on my star quest."

The Silent Master smiled back, and kept silent.

"I am on a mission to save my friend, the Moth. I understand you are the Master of Right Speech, so I will be eternally grateful for anything that you can teach me that will help me."

The Silent Master smiled and kept mum.

The tiny Fireball didn't know what to do and just stood there, feeling dumb.

Then she noticed, the Master was actually sitting in a lotus posture on the ground, perhaps in meditation right before she appeared. In front of him, at a comfortable distance, another meditation mat was laid out on the floor.

She remembered how she was told to meditate at her previous two stars, so she figured things are escalating now.

She smiled and got into a lotus posture in front of the silent master. She was uncomfortable, her feet were not used to being in this pose, and her spine was not used to sitting on the floor, but with a little adjustment she was relatively comfortable. She saw the Master was meditating with his eyes closed, so she closed her eyes.

First her mind jumped around, topic to topic, then slowly, she was able to take charge of it and guide it to where she wanted it to focus - the present moment. She asked herself - What do I have to learn here? Then after a brief contemplation, she refined her question to - What do I need to learn here?

In meditation, one enters a dimension where time and space does not exist, so she didn't know how long she spent in that state.

When she opened her eyes, the Silent Master was looking at her, smiling.

That's when she realised what she had noticed when she first landed on this star but could not put it in words.

There was a divine silence in the air.

Sounds of nature could be heard, but there was nothing else.

As she was admiring this divine silence, she heard the most beautiful voice in the universe singing an unheard tune.

Next moment, she realised it wasn't singing, it just sounded so beautiful and pure because it was so rare and precious. It was her new Master speaking to her.

The Silent Master said, "I have two words for you."

As he spoke, the smile never left his face, "Silence and Truth."

Then his lips rested again, and the smile became even more beautiful.

The tiny Fireball closed her eyes and let those words get absorbed in her being. Even though she didn't understand them fully yet, she recognised them for the treasure they were, for they were spoken by someone who lived in silence.

She meditated a few moments longer then decided to leave. The Silent Master had given her all she needed from him. No more words were needed.

She took a silent bow and retreated.

She couldn't be sure, but she felt she saw her master's smile widen as his hands were raised to bless her journey onward.

She was grateful.

SIGNAL 9

Display a square flag with a ball below it.

Noble Star #4

Right conduct is to live for others.
To give our everything in service of existence.

— FROM THE TRAVEL DIARIES OF THE
TINY FIREBALL.

The tiny Fireball met the fourth star keeper who was like a grandma who pretended to love knitting, but had a secret bad-ass hobby. In case of this grandma, it was gardening, or rather forestry, and she was clearly gifted at that. She exuded the energy of a loving grandma, the aura that accompanies an old, weathered soul, but her physical form radiated youthfulness of prime, like the vegetation around her.

THE TINY FIREBALL

The fourth star was covered in a lush forest full of starlit trees, bushes, orchards, gardens, vines and celestial flowers. The kindly grandma had planted a lot of love and sweat on this star.

The tiny Fireball just felt like playing here, swinging from the vines, climbing trees, playing explorer. Then she reminded herself this wasn't a social visit.

"You look famished," the Gifted Gardener spoke to her first. Then she plucked a ripe plum and handed it to the tiny visitor.

The tiny Fireball felt the smooth, delicate skin of the plum, then brought it close to her nose. It smelt of a sweet summer morning. She took a bite and her tastebuds were immediately in love with the juicy tang. It instantly rejuvenated her.

"Such kind creatures, right?" the Gifted Gardener said admiring her plants.

The tiny Fireball nodded as she gobbled up the plum. She did not know she was so hungry.

"The entire plant kingdom gives and gives and gives. Everything it has, it sacrifices for everything else. The silent sacrifice it makes speaks of a quiet wisdom. It nourishes the needy across the universe."

The tiny Fireball finished the plum and put the pit on the ground near her feet and, as was her habit, covered it with soil.

The Gifted Gardener said, "By divine law and justice, it is nourished back in turn."

The tiny Fireball smiled.

"That's the thing about this Universe. Anything and everything you give it, it brings it back to you, often multiplied. The plant kingdom thrives by giving. And in this same universe some try to thrive by clinging and hoarding. To sacrifice everything we have is to gain everything we need."

The tiny Fireball smiled. She hadn't said a word, she had been practising what the Silent Master had taught her, and without a word, she had picked up such gems from the Gifted Gardener - the Keeper of the Star of Right Conduct.

The Gardener smiled and packed a basket of her juiciest fruits for the tiny Fireball.

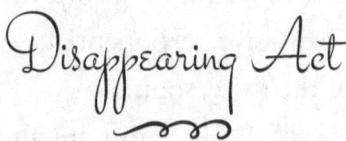

Disappearing Act

I could see my breath. It came out as little clouds and drifted away, blending into the mist. We were huddled close aboard our floating palace, me and the tiny Fireball.

The blankets, quilts and sweaters we had were the invisible kind, and pretty as they were, they were not certified for their warmth.

I thought maybe we are drifting closer to the poles, north or south I could toss a coin and tell you.

"So, with every star-hop, you shrink in size?"

"Nearly by half," said the tiny Fireball.

"So, you must have been enormous when you started your journey."

"My home star is one of the largest stars in the Universe. You can imagine its size by imagining how big I must have been when I started on my star quest, and the fact that, even back there, I was know as the 'tiny' Fireball."

"That is huge!" I knew how the compounding principle worked, when things go up by a factor of two, the growth is explosive, exponential. When things are shrinking to half their size, soon...

"Wait a second," I said, "You are already so tiny and you have one more star to get to right?"

"Right."

"You'll be so small, you'll disappear completely!" I said and burst out laughing.

The tiny Fireball contemplated my words in her silence and said, "Perhaps."

Today, as I am telling you about it, I imagine I can read her thoughts in that moment.

If I were to disappear, what will happen to my mission? Who will save my Moth?

SIGNAL 10

Radiotelephone alarm - Transmit two sinusoidal audio frequency tones (2200 Hertz and 1300 Hertz) for a duration of 30 to 60 seconds. (Technical knowledge + equipment needed)

Noble Star #5

Right living is right doing.
   We are what we have done.
   What we do, we will become.
   All Life is One Life.

— FROM THE TRAVEL DIARIES OF THE
TINY FIREBALL.

The next star hop started the same, tremendous acceleration, intense heat, smooth landing and signature shrinkage; but it ended with the tiny Fireball in a classroom presided by the star keeper who was a wise, young professor.

The class was full, the young professor must be quite popular. He was also a Squirrel.

That's how the tiny Fireball knew she wasn't dreaming, only the real universe could be so wonky.

She looked around at her fellow students. If there is ever a UN assembly for the universe, this is what it would look like she thought and chuckled.

A chalk flew in her direction.

"Quiet, back there!" Her chuckle had betrayed her in the quiet classroom. Other students looked at her disapproving. Embarrassed, she sunk further into her seat, wishing the bench would swallow her whole.

"As I was saying," the Squirrel Professor continued, "Immortality is now accessible. And since there is no other time in the universe than now, it has always been accessible."

"So how do we attain it?" a student voice came in from some corner. The tiny Fireball perked up too, immortality is the perfect solution to her Moth's problem.

The Squirrel Professor continued, "To attain immortality, life that knows no end, you have to learn Right Living first. The first tenet of it is to cause no harm to any other being. All life is one life. If you hurt another, guess who are you hurting?"

The Squirrel Professor was expounding virtues through his buck teeth, but he looked nothing but adorable to the tiny Fireball. She had just been inducted into the innocent, universal tradition of crushing on your teacher. Then, the object of her affections started speaking of love.

"The way to love is love. Don't be in love. Practise love. What we love, we practise, what we practise, we become. That's right living."

"Love can never be scarce, for it lies within you. You are the great fountain of love and wisdom. The same thing that created this universe has created you, it dreams through you, achieves through you, lives through you and experiences itself through you. Whatever it is, you are. When you are able to recognise and demonstrate this in your life, you'll have realised yourself. When you do all you can to bring others into this realisation, you'll be doing the right work which will lead you into Right Living."

The bell rang, class was over. Without wasting a second, the students gathered their belongings and clamoured out. Different star systems, different species, different beings, still the universe was more alike than different.

A bit conscious, thanks to the butterflies in her stomach, the tiny Fireball approached the Squirrel Professor's desk. He was shoving his notes in his bag as she said, "Sir, I have a question…"

"I cannot tell you the dates for the surprise test…" said the Squirrel Professor and snapped his bag shut.

"No, no… I have a different question."

The Squirrel Professor stared at her through his rimmed bifocals.

"I am learning a lot of things on my star quest, things that sound deep and important..."

"But?"

"But, I honestly don't know what it all means! How will I be able to save my friend? I have been to five stars and I am nowhere close to my answer. What do I do?"

Something softened in the Squirrel Professor's eyes and he said, "This is exactly how it works. You'll find the answer you need, but it won't magically land on your lap. You'll have to work for it. All your classmates have different goals, all of them want different things, but they all learnt the same handful of general things I spoke about."

"The raw material is the same, when you apply this knowledge, these truths to your unique situation, your solution will emerge from them. You'll only gather timber on your star quest, the fire will be lit by something within you, that's greater than you."

The tiny Fireball smiled. There was something greater within this Star Keeper that was shining through the small stature.

She knew she had learnt all the Noble Star #5, and its star keeper the Squirrel Professor had to teach her.

She offered her eternal gratitude to the professor who had in seconds transformed from being a teacher crush to one of her revered masters.

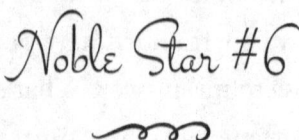

Right Effort is to live less and less for ourselves.
By living less and less for itself, a part assumes the full quality of the Whole.

— FROM THE TRAVEL DIARIES OF THE
TINY FIREBALL.

The tiny Fireball was ready this time. Before she arrived at the sixth Noble star, she had a smaller dress and shoes ready, preparing them was a refreshing change between her meditations.

However, she was not prepared to find herself in the backseat of a cab upon landing. This was her first landing where long after touchdown she was still moving, barrelling down the freeway of a strange new land. Everything was a beautiful blur outside her passenger side window. She saw neon shop lights streaking past, galactic museums that had actual stars hanging overhead as spotlights, a broadway theatre smack in the middle of a business district, were a few of the things she could identify as she flew past them in her taxicab.

She turned to the driver and said, "Excuse me sir..."

The taxi driver said, "Yes love?"

Love? The tiny Fireball thought, have I landed in an alternate Great Britain by mistake?

"I think I have landed at the wrong address... exactly, where am I?"

"The Star of Right Effort of course, although I think it should be rebranded as the Star of Perfection... I would never take you to the wrong place."

"Okay, I think the landscape threw me off... so, I am at the right place. Great, could you take me to the Star Keeper please?"

"No, I cannot."

"Why not? You are a taxi driver, taking people where they want to go is what you do."

"Well, thank you for explaining me my job," he was smiling when he said it. A lesser being would have mistaken the tiny Fireball's words to be offensive, but he was wise enough to see that she meant no disrespect but was merely curious.

Still smiling, he said, "I can't take you to the Star

Keeper because you are already with him."

The tiny Fireball did a double take fit for meme, and looked at the driver carefully.

There was a quiet radiance about him. She saw the taxi was impeccable, cushions comfortable and interiors smelled of fresh lilies and sandalwood. While they were speeding through the star, sometimes on freeways, sometimes through the city streets, they were following every road sign, speed limit and the right of way. The car never creaked, nor moaned at undue strain put on her fine machinery, everything was well oiled and performing to perfection.

She was being driven in a taxicab by a Master indeed.

She bowed and said, "Forgive me, I should have guessed."

The smile on his weathered face spread to his eyes and he said, "Quiet alright, love."

"You already know, why I am here?"

"I sure do."

"If I still ask you about it, you'll say 'I already know the answer', correct?"

He laughed.

The tiny Fireball joined in, his laughter felt like warming your palms on a cup of hot chocolate on a rainy winter morning.

"Fine, let's just drive around and chat then. I think you'll tell me all I need to know and I will do my best to half understand it... at best."

He laughed louder, then said, "You really ought to give yourself more credit. You are smarter than you know and you are making more progress than your realise. You have Divinity within you, let it shine forth."

"You are too kind."

"I speak the truth."

"So, tell me, why do you want to rename your star?"

"Star of Right Effort is good too, but I feel the result of it is Perfection. When we let our Divinity shine forth, when we let the wisdom within speak and act through us, what results is a life of pure perfection. So, I think the result of right actions would have made a much stronger brand name. I am reading a book on marketing and it says, people don't buy a drill or a hole, they buy the feeling of having a beautiful nail hanging on their walls... or something like it."

It was the tiny Fireball's turn to break into laughter, and the taxi driver Star Keeper joined in, like a true sport.

"If you ever run a petition, I will sign it."

"Thanks for your support! You know, there's pure perfection within us. You are the Ruler of the Universe, you don't realise it yet, you don't accept it yet, because you have not experienced it yet. The only way to experience it is to raise your vibration. Think great thoughts. Live on a high level of greatness. Descend not to selfishness in any form. The more we live for others, the more we live for the whole of existence, the higher we rise. Living for others means serving others who have less than we have and know less than we know."

"Think of Love. You solve the secret of existence if Love directs you into Right Effort of its expression. The Wisdom of the Universe is at work within you and it will Light your way when your actions are motivated by Love. And True Love is Self Less."

The tiny Fireball was quietly making mental notes.

"You are everything that is, the Whole. There is no need for the whole to live unto itself, its mission is to live for the parts, which know less than the whole. By living less and less for itself, the Part assumes the full quality and nature of the Whole, losing itself in the life of the Whole. All this is nice to read, nice to say, nice to hear, nice to think, but we are what we DO. Doing requires effort. When our doing is motivated by Love and directed by the Divine Wisdom within us, every action we take is considered as Right Effort."

The tiny Fireball looked at the radiant face of this Master, the impeccable taxi and the perfection of the cityscape blurring outside her window. Everything here was created by someone, and she could see the perfection in the results. She knew if the perfection was present in the results, it would have been present in the efforts behind them. The rebranding would fit it perfectly.

As if hearing her thoughts, the Master taxi driver smiled and stopped the meter.

Her ride had come to an end.

SIGNAL 11

Display code flags November, Charlie.

Outlandish

To be fair and honest, there were many times when I found the tiny Fireball's travel stories works of an active imagination. I mean, come on, Squirrel Professors, melting moonstones with thought, Star Keepers that ferry passengers in taxicabs... absolute bonkers, right?

Except, outlandish as her stories were, there was something in those encounters that resonated with me like nothing but the truth does. Something was shifting in me as something was shifting in her as she experienced them. Besides, who was I to judge? Here I was in the middle of the ocean, always a moment away from a hungry shark or my own thirst or hunger eager to wipe out my whole existence with a gross yet satisfying burp. And as I confronted my mortality every day, I was spending those same days with a cute, tiny little creature that could not exist in the universe I had previously known. Yet, here she was, and here I was with her.

Dr Wadeson is going to have a field day trying to decode these tales when I dump them on him. I laughed out loud at that thought. The tiny Fireball was sleeping close by, but I wasn't afraid of waking her up. She always said, waking up to laughter was one of the best ways to wake up. As I was thinking of the new mansion Dr Wadeson will surely be able to build thanks to his favourite patient, I suddenly paused, leaving an unfinished laugh hanging in the air.

This was the first time since my second shipwreck that I had thought of my life beyond this raft.

Strange.

I looked at the tiny Fireball. She was still sleeping, but I could have sworn I saw a flicker of a smile pass on her face.

Noble Star #7

Right Meditation is the key to the Palace of Wisdom Within and the Celestial Kingdom.

— FROM THE TRAVEL DIARIES OF THE TINY FIREBALL.

The tiny Fireball arrived at her next stop, the Noble Star #7. The vibe here was in stark contrast to the bustling metropolis and city streets of her previous star.

She found herself by a gently flowing river stream. The air carried sweetness from orchards just beyond the horizon. The day felt pleasantly warm on her skin and breeze swayed her in its lap. There was a relatively large, unassuming tree beside the stream with vines reaching to the earth below, while her branches were getting ready to touch the heavens above. There was no one else in sight, no one to ask for directions. The tiny Fireball was weary from her travels.

She had covered much distance, met many Masters, learnt a great deal, yet she didn't have a definite answer on how to save her Moth.

Her lovely friend, the colourful, adventurous, goofy Moth.

She was close to the end of her star quest. She had shrunk so much, she was a shade away from being invisible. Would she be able to make the journey back to her home star in this state? Her thoughts seemed heavy on her tiny shoulders. She decided to do what had served her best on this journey so far. To sit down and meditate, to look for the answers within.

She found a comfortable spot in the tree's shade by the stream, sat down cross-legged, rested her eyes and eased into meditation.

She felt the light of wisdom and love rise within her and flood her being.

"Welcome to my star."

She was startled to hear the voice and was about to open her eyes, when she realised, the voice had not spoken out loud. It was spoken to her silently, in her meditation.

This was a private dialogue.

The voice continued, "I am happy that the first act you have done on the Star of Right Meditation, is to sit down and meditate."

"You are the Star Keeper?"

"That's right."

"But who and where are you? I was scanning the star from the sky even before I landed and I didn't see you anywhere."

"You have seen me. It's in my shade that you are sitting right now."

"Ah, you are the tree. I thought you looked ordinary and majestic at the same time."

"I am the tree alright, and I don't know about majestic or anything, but yes, a lot of Masters have rested and meditated in my shade on their way to the Celestial Kingdom. I believe, they call me the Bodhi tree in some parts of the Universe."

"I have heard about you! What an honour..." the tiny Fireball was happy to meet one so revered across the Universe.

The inner dialogue continued while the tiny Fireball sat there under the shade of the Bodhi tree. She said, "I want to meditate deeply but my thoughts are riddled with worry over my friend and her safety..."

The Bodhi tree said, "Worry has a purpose, learning to discard it. While you have travelled here to save your friend, you have also been led here to learn how to meditate in the right way. Right Meditation is the state of mind at peace, when without any preconceived notions, you can see things as they are."

"When you practise meditation, in deepest humility,

you are led to the unfoldment of the Truth of your Being, and to the truth of Every Living Thing, of which you are a part."

"There is no other way. Go within. Know your mortality, but also know that you have entered the battlefield of life to meet your immortality. Conduct yourself as an immortal among mortals. Let your Light Shine."

"Do what you have to do with the greatest joy, knowing that which is Eternal is doing it through you."

"When you are successful in meditation, you will establish a spiritual contact with the Higher Ones. Multiple intelligences co-exist in our Universe. Bumblebees have a certain degree of intelligence, humans another, relatively higher level of intelligence. Similarly, there are intelligences higher than our own present all around us, silently urging us forward and onwards to higher achievements on all planes of life."

"The purpose of Right Meditation is to break down the Prison cells of Illusion that seem to fill our world and reveal the Palace of Wisdom that has been hidden from us. The Secrets of Life are hidden from us, but they are always within our reach. Meditation is your key to this Palace and the Celestial Kingdom."

"The Illusions are powerful, they have ruled over you all your life, their roots run deep. That's why you need to be steadfast in your meditation, the task before you is not an easy one, but consistent Right Meditation makes it easy."

"The Higher Ones are ever ready and waiting to help you, but wise as they are, they know only to help those who first help themselves. The illusions will always try to bind you a false reality. When you stand your ground, when you demonstrate your intent to go beyond them through the purity of your thoughts and actions, applying everything you have learnt on your journey, the gateway will open for you. The Higher Ones will make sure it does. It all begins with you."

"This is easy enough to understand intellectually for the one who has travelled some distance on the Path, but to spiritually know it, you have to LIVE it, experience it. What is told is forgotten, what is experienced is ingrained in our memory forevermore."

The tiny Fireball was carefully storing away the words of the Bodhi tree in her consciousness like the priceless gems they were. She meditated upon them in her own silence. Some understanding was dawning within her but it was still lying just beyond the horizon of her consciousness. All in good time, she thought.

She must have been sitting there for a few moments or for a millennium, she didn't know, time passed differently in meditation, but soon she realised, the Bodhi tree was quiet for a while, having imparted her wisdom.

Without moving a muscle or uttering a sound, in her Divine Silence, the tiny Fireball bowed to the Mighty

Fount of Knowledge that had its roots stretching to eternity and offered her loving gratitude.

After meditating for so long on her journey, she was finally on the path of Right Meditation.

The Bodhi tree smiled in the wind and rained some of her most beautiful petals on the tiny Meditator.

SIGNAL 12

Turn on the Position Indicating Radio beacon.

A Logistical Problem

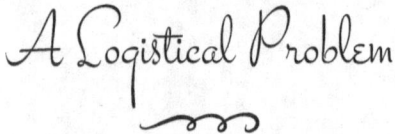

"Who is your Moth?" the tiny Fireball asked me one day.

"No one," I said and then laughed and added, "Maybe you."

She shook her head and said, "So you just haven't met... yet. You will."

I laughed some more. I had given up on my Moth, if she even existed, clearly we were both too jaded to look for each other.

Nothing had brought light to my days like the tiny Fireball had in this bleak place.

I wanted the tiny Fireball to win. I wanted her to succeed in her star quest. She never admitted it, but I knew it was love that had sent her hopping and hurtling across the universe at immense peril to herself.

Every star jump came with great pain, and yet, she

brushed over it as if it was nothing. Every star hop left her diminished, frailer, to the point that when I met her, she was barely discernible to the eye. She had zero complaints though. Anything for her Moth.

Rare was such love, the kind not bonded by blood, but by souls, by something that transcends life. A love that I was certain I will never know.

So, I wanted her quest to be successful - so that, even if not in my own life, love somewhere may be successful. For the first time in my life, I found myself brooding less over my misfortunes and brainstorming more with her on her quest.

Apparently, the last jump was key now. She had been to the 7 Nobles, learnt a lot, meditated a lot, but she was nowhere close to a definite way of saving her Moth. The last star would have the answer.

There was a logistical problem though.

Every jump she had made, she had made from a star. The star's energy, the sheer force it packed had propelled her jumps. It was no easy matter, hopping from star to star. Just like a rocket leaving earth, great amount of energy was required, the kind not available on a planet 70% covered by water. All of earth's available energy sources put together would not be enough.

There has to be a way. The tiny Fireball always said - In an infinite Universe, whatever can be imagined, is.

So, I put my imagination and all parts of my being to work. I was going to find the way for her to succeed.

I was filled with joy. My resolution to help her had lifted my spirits, I was smiling. Even the tiny Fireball noticed and smiled back at me, reading my intentions behind it.

The joy was short-lived.

For, that very moment a powerful wave battered and washed over the raft. I lost my balance, but after a quick stumble, regained my footing. The tiny Fireball was in my hand, resting in her peanut butter jar, so she was safe. But my miracle maker was gone.

My Miracle Maker

You may have wondered how did I survive so long onboard my raft without drinking water. The credit goes to my Miracle maker, which was part of the standard issue 'Survival kit' securely strapped to my raft.

It's a small apparatus that uses the sun's heat to evaporate sea water and convert it into drinking water, using the simple process taught in grade schools. It gives you two things, salt which, after hunger, is a great seasoning, and it gives you life sustaining juice of Mother Earth.

As long as you have this water maker, sun shining overhead and plenty of supply of seawater, you will never die of thirst in middle of the sea — in theory.

The reality is, the process is painfully slow. At times, the sun doesn't shine. Sometimes, it can take days to fill a glass. With the seas's violent swings, sometimes, salt water gets mixed in with fresh water... you get the idea. A million things can go wrong with it, and they often do. So, in spite of having it, I was usually thirsty.

I was grateful to have it though. It had kept me alive for months now. Without it, I would have perished long ago. Man can go for weeks without food, but will not last a week without water - that's why I called it my Miracle maker.

Now, it was gone. Swallowed by the sea. Perhaps I had stolen more than my fair share from it, and now, the sea was extracting a ransom.

I had to act fast. I had to figure out a way of getting the tiny Fireball on her way soon. Love must prevail. I had to save her at any cost.

The final countdown had begun.

Destination Sol

Even as my throat was running dry, my mind was racing. I was thinking of ways of getting the tiny Fireball some new fuel source.

"How about tidal energy? Our scientists use it to generate electricity, perhaps you can use it to propel your space jump?"

The tiny Fireball smiled and thanked me for my latest creative suggestion, and then politely dismissed it, like all others before it.

"How far is your next star anyway? What is it called?"

"Noble Star #8 is the Star of Right Rapture. It's not too far from here actually, it's also known as Sol in some parts of the Universe."

I gasped. "No way! Your next star is the Earth's Sun? It's right there, shining down on us," I pointed.

The tiny Fireball said, "I know. That's what brought

me close to you. I was en route to it when I saw you adrift and decided to land here."

"Wait a second!" I was shocked at this revelation, "You saw me from outer space and *decided* to land on my raft? Instead of going to the one place in the universe that could save the love of your life? Why did you do that? Why??"

A soft smile and silence were the only answers I received.

That night, I lay awake looking at the stars and thinking of the morning when the tiny Fireball appeared on my raft.

It was right after the night I made an extraordinary decision.

Coincidence?

I thought — there aren't any.

Launch a parachute with a Red Flare.

An Extraordinary Decision

Remember how, right at the beginning, I told you that newspapers had proven with experts and statistics and charts that the probability of me being in another shipwreck was practically zero?

There's another side to it, another conclusion of the same charts. No one had spoken about it, but it dawned on me before I met the tiny Fireball, a few weeks into my second shipwreck.

The probability of me surviving another shipwreck was practically zero too.

No one gets that lucky.

I was going to die this time.

When I realised this, I shrugged. There was no resentment. I had been living a lonely life and now I was going to die a lonely death. Like a raft passing in the night.

A pathetic, unsatisfying climax to match the life I had been leading.

That's when I made an extraordinary decision.

I decided to do it on my terms.

My life so far had been a consequence of fate, circumstances, choices of other people. My exit, my last act, the grand finale would be written by me.

I decided to throw myself a grand send off party.

Then I thought, you can't have a party without some supplies, so I scanned my raft. Some items in my standard issue 'Survival kit' could work. There were food rations, a fishing line, a flare gun with a couple of rounds, a map to navigate by the stars, the water purifier and a few other trinkets. Yeah, it will do.

Tonight, my raft is going to be hosting the most epic party in the universe.

I was startled to hear a madman roaring in laughter and looked around my raft.

There was no one else, just me, laughing.

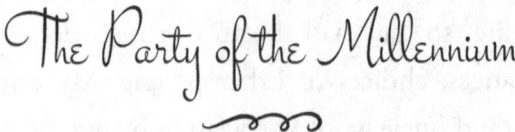

The Party of the Millennium

The sky was burning. The protesting colours had just broken into a riot, and the clouds were desperately trying to restore order.

That last sunset was something.

Most men cower and run from death all their lives. It's a subject they find too heavy, too confusing, they feel helpless in front of it, so they do their best to avoid it. Just like everything you try to run from and avoid, it is always a step behind you, ready to pounce in an unguarded moment, lurking in the shadows because your fear puts it there.

I had no such reservations.

You are only averse to death if you have something to look forward to in life.

I had lived my life looking backward.

I was ready.

For weeks I had been careful with my supplies, rationing everything, knowing from my first experience that nothing kills your spirit like thirst and hunger.

I had planned to stretch my rations out, eating only on the brink of absolute famine, drinking water when I was parched, hoarding everything possible.

But this was a party.

Parties are a definition of excess.

So, I stuffed my face and emptied the cans. There was no DJ, no speakers, no LPs or playlists, so I sang me some songs. I sang, I yelled, there were no neighbours asking to keep it down.

These days no self-respecting party is complete without trust, relationships, or at least things getting broken, so I ripped the navigation guide and tossed the pages in the air.

At some point, I started dancing. There was nothing I could eat, drink or smoke that was intoxicating on board my raft, but I was delirious.

To me, this was the party of the millennium.

It needed fireworks. I grabbed the flare gun and set it off, burning through all the rounds in quick succession.

The flares looked gorgeous in the night sky.

If there was a ship nearby, it could spot the flare signal, but there wasn't a soul around to spoil my plans.

Just as my delirium peaked, highlights of my life

flashed before my eyes. There was nothing in there to make me change my mind.

I was done.

The Second Extraordinary Decision

The next morning the tiny Fireball appeared on my raft. My suspicions were confirmed near the end. It was no coincidence.

Over 70% of Earth is covered by water.

While it is easy to see it on a flat, two-dimensional map of the world, in reality as Earth revolves around its axis in 3 dimensions, we only ever see half of it. The other half is hidden from our vision.

Our land mass and oceans are placed such that, from one particular angle in space, our planet appears to be completely covered in water. Hence the earned nick-name, the blue planet.

That's how the tiny Fireball first saw me.

THE TINY FIREBALL

My party flares caught her eye as she was en route to the last stop on her star quest - Sol, also known as the Earth's Sun. She saw me bobbing on a battered raft, a small dot in the vast blue.

No joy, no land, no hope in sight.

She could sense immense sadness radiating from my tiny raft. She saw me, a creature alien to love, sans affection, on the brink, a flame soon to be exhausted forever.

She looked up beyond the horizon, to the Sun. It was her final stop, the Noble Star #8. The key to saving her Moth, her lovely, lovely Moth. All she had to do was keep going and the Noble Star will impart wisdom and provide a solution to save her beloved.

Then she would return to her home star and be with her dear friend, forever. All that she had ever desired was within reach. Just keep going, a part of her told her.

She sighed.

How could she ignore the life in front of her to save a life somewhere else in the universe?

She set her destination for my raft.

Thanks to all the star hopping business, by now she was feeble, a tiny little thing, barely a spark. She decided to join me, a worthless, ungrateful stranger, in the middle of the sea. She decided to join me on a planet, that from her perspective, was made of nothing but the sea. An ocean of a planet that could wipe out her existence with a careless shrug or an intentional sigh.

She wasn't just risking herself. With her, any hopes for her Moth would be lost forever. Knowing this, she chose to help me, to try to save me.

She valued my worthless life over her love.

The second extraordinary decision of the night was made.

SIGNAL
14

Broadcast 'Mayday' on Radio.

The Desire to Live

I lay on the floor of my raft, withering in pain. If there was any disposable water left in my body, it would have gushed through my eyes, but I was nearing a week since I had drunk any water. The physical pains I was experiencing were staggering, reminiscent of unspoken terrors witnessed by medieval dungeons, but something else hurt me more.

My heart.

The tiny Fireball had just finished telling me how and why she joined me on my raft.

I knew she needed a star's heat and energy to propel her space jumps. That was her fuel, something that planet Earth did not, could not ever have, because it was not a star.

There was simply no way for her to continue on her

star quest and no way for her to return to her home star, and I was responsible for all of it. If only I would have implemented my extraordinary decision, without throwing my crazy party, she would have been with the love of her life by now.

She tried to save me, and while she had brought colour back into my life, rekindled the desire in my heart to live again, here I was, dying anyway.

It had all been in vain, and I was responsible. I knew about her challenges earlier, and I always wanted her to succeed, but it was not really my problem.

We were both caught in an unfortunate situation... so I thought.

Now I knew, she was here for me. She chose to be with me. My life was mine to throw away, my death was mine to choose, but now, I was responsible for hers.

"Stop it..." she said, reading my thoughts, "it was my decision, and it was a wise one."

I looked at her, even in our final moments together, she was trying to ease my burdens, what a special thing she was, more human than some of the actual humans I had encountered.

She smiled and said, "We meet what we are. By the way, tell me more about wanting to live again... what would you do?"

"No use thinking about it," I said, "We are never making out of this ocean alive."

"Still, tell a friend, will you?"

How could I say no to that? I looked at the setting sun and sighed, it was better to talk about pleasant things in your final moments.

"I would make it count. Build my world within this world. Do something useful, you know. All my life I have drifted, like I am drifting on this raft - aimless, purposeless. I would like to contribute to the world somehow. Be there for the people who show up in my life, like you have been here for me. I don't want to run a charity or anything, nothing that noble or extreme, I just want to be a good human being... in my own way. Just help bring some more light into this world."

The darkness dispersed and the light was returning to my eyes.

"I would like to share the kind of selfless love and kindness you have shown me over the past few months."

The tiny Fireball smiled and nuzzled close to me, like a child sleeps in a mother's embrace.

She was content.

Although she had failed in her star quest, although she would never visit the Noble Star #8, although she may never see her Moth again, she had at least awakened my desire to live and love again. She felt in a small way, she had succeeded.

She felt this was probably why the universe had sent her to my raft, to save me from myself. She could rest easy now, perhaps even figure out how to continue on her journey. Her work here was done.

She was wrong.

Our final horror was yet to come.

Before that, came a visitor.

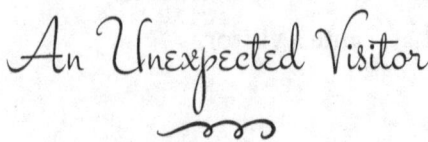
An Unexpected Visitor

To do what you have to do with the greatest joy is to demonstrate that the Highest is doing it through you.

Unconditional Love is the eternal fuel that drives Life and this Universe.

— FROM THE TRAVEL DIARIES OF THE
TINY FIREBALL.

That night, the tiny Fireball dreamed. In her dreams, she welcomed an unexpected guest into her mind.

"Well, hello there!" his voice boomed as his presence lit up her inner world.

"Um... hi?" the tiny Fireball said, trying to gather her bearings. Dreams could be disorienting.

"Sorry, I let myself in, I hope you don't mind. The door was open," he said, pointing to a door the tiny Fireball could swear wasn't there a moment ago. There were no walls around it, it was just a freestanding door in a beautiful garden. What purpose could it serve, except give this stranger an excuse to saunter right in. The door disappeared with a flourish. This visitor was some kind of magician.

He said, "I believe you have been trying to reach me."

The tiny Fireball gasped, "No way! You are not..."

"Sol. The one and only... Although, I go with many names. Sol. Sun. Suraj, Suryaa... it's a long list, I could bring you a copy if you want?"

The tiny Fireball was speechless, but she recovered quickly and bowed. "You are the Star keeper of Noble Star #8. Wow, I have been planning to visit you for a long time..."

"I know. I also know why you got delayed... that was mighty nice of you, by the way."

The tiny Fireball beamed.

"Since you were indisposed, I decided to visit you instead. I hope it is alright?"

"Of course, welcome to my Dream World."

"Thanks, so, tell me, how can I help?"

"I want to learn how to save my friend, my Moth..."

The Star Keeper was much like the tiny Fireball, a being of sheer luminance, with no discerning shape or features, yet somehow it was easy to know when he was smiling, like he was now, his light grew brighter.

He said, "As you have learned my dear, we Star Keepers speak in vague generalities, kind of an annoying quirk of ours, if I am being honest," he smiled and winked. "But, we give you all the clues you need and point you in the right direction. So that you can figure out the answers your own way. We find that works the best. So, I cannot give a straight answer to your question, but I can help. Will that be okay?"

"Of course, I understand. Life doesn't give us solutions like instant noodles. It gives us the power and the wisdom to build ourselves, so we can find solutions using the knowledge we have been given."

The Sol star keeper smiled and said, "I see that you have traveled well."

They started walking on clouds.

"As you know, they call me the Star of Right Rapture. Exaltation, euphoria, bliss, there are many definitions, what I really identify the most with is Unconditional Love. The substance of the Eternal, the Absolute, the ALL that is, the Everlasting, is Love."

"What is Love? It is something that can't be defined in words, but it can be known in silence, through practise. We can only know it by its effects. Love is the Spirit of Life. Love is Wisdom. Love is Light. We must live for Love, we must die for Love, for only in Love do we find Resurrection, which is Right Rapture. Create a Kingdom of Light within and you create a Kingdom of Light everywhere. You are the Creator of everything that was, is and will be."

They had reached the end of the road and both were gleaming brighter than they ever had. It was a gift to be in the presence.

The tiny Fireball bowed and accepted the loving blessings of the brightest star in the galaxy.

She knew she had just learnt something important. Something that will help her save her Moth. Like all the wisdom in the world, it was handed to her as a riddle. She was confident that with enough time to meditate over it, she will find the way to a happily ever after.

She didn't know it yet, but we were hours away from absolute doom.

The Calm

The next morning the tiny Fireball told me all about her dream visitor.

"This is amazing! So, you might be the first one who completed her star quest without actually travelling to all the eight stars, that's awesome!"

She smiled. We were both so excited.

"So, now you can travel back to your home star and be with your Moth..." I said the words and immediately, I was touched by grief. It meant saying goodbye to my one friend in this desolate place.

"I'm not leaving you alone," she said smiling, "Besides, I could have travelled easily back if I had visited Sol, because then, I could have used the star's energy to propel my space jump. Sol visited me instead, kind of him to do so, of course. In my dream, I could only access his wisdom, not his energy. So, without any fuel source, I am just as stranded on this raft as you are."

Reality. Shucks.

Suddenly all the fatigue and the ache and the hunger and the thirst, all came back. The tiny Fireball's bit of good news had washed it all to the background, but now it was back on the centre stage.

I was dying here, and unless we figured out a way to get the tiny Fireball into the orbit again, she was going to perish here as well. I shrugged the dark thoughts aside, focussed on the light and said, "At least, technically your star quest is now complete."

"In a way. I haven't figured out how to save my Moth yet."

"You'll figure it out."

"Do you think my Moth would still be there waiting for me? What if she got bored and ventured to another star? Or grew impatient and headed to the surface of my home star??"

The darkness was getting to her too.

I shooed it away. "No way. From what you've told me of your Moth, she's way too smart to do any of that. She'll be fine, you'll see. I bet she throws you in her arms the minute she sees you."

"We hugged once you know," the tiny Fireball said, eyes sparkling through the darkness, "it hurt me because it hurt her. But, it was the most beautiful thing in the world."

I smiled, and quietly let her live the memory.

I focused on the sound of the gentle waves caressing our raft. It was wonderfully relaxing moment, that calm before the storm.

Before this beautiful day was over, the sea and our life raft would have merged into one.

Smoke.
Flames on the vessel.

The Storm

"I solved the mystery."

I tried to focus on the tiny Fireball's words. I had been drifting in and out of consciousness. My body, deprived of all the essential materials it needed to survive, was shutting down everything that wasn't life supporting to conserve what it could. Every bit mattered.

The tiny Fireball said, "I figured out why I kept getting smaller and smaller with every star jump."

"Why?"

"As we keep going inwards, studying the knowledge we have uncovered, we start losing all the false beliefs, the pain, the base and the profane we have accumulated all our lives. When we are able to detach and simply observe all this gross matter, without judging, without classifying it as good or bad, it starts fading away. The gross leaves, the subtle remains. The Divinity within us is made of subtle matter, that's why we feel light, the essential energies of the universe are light, and ever so soft. That's why, all the timeless wisdom in the world advocates letting go. As we let go, we grow lighter, and the more readily we flow with the Universe. The way of the universe is always better than my way or your way," she added with a chuckle, "or the highway."

I smiled and said, "Okay, if you say so." I had no intentions of taxing my brain by thinking over her words, when speaking was a strain. She was usually right about these things, so I simply trusted her.

I could see that she had been meditating, and it was clearly working. Good for her.

Meanwhile, I could feel with unquestioning certainty that my water grave was almost ready.

I laughed at the timing.

Right when this little odd stranger had rekindled my desire to live, my life was ebbing away from me.

It was exactly 9.55 pm when a deckhand, eager to prove himself on his maiden mission, spotted a signal onboard INS Vikrant.

The Captain, Mr Singh, a gentle giant of a man who had already signed out and retired for the day, was notified. He hurried to the starboard clutching his untied robe shut with one hand and a pair of binoculars in another. In the sea of darkness, far on the horizon, he saw something that had no business being there.

A small fire.

The sentry was right. It was a distress call, perhaps from a small fishing boat that had veered way off course.

Immediately, he bellowed orders to his troops, who promptly jumped into action at the speed only Indian Navy does. In the next 42 seconds, a rubber speedboat, with engines strong enough to run down pirates, smugglers and insurgents, was chopping water as it headed towards the dwindling fire.

A lot slower compared to the speedboat, but still faster than most commercial ships, the pride of the Indian Naval Fleet, INS Vikrant, an aircraft carrier, turned course, and followed the speedboat as per Mr Singh's commands. The distance to the target was 9.6 nautical miles.

Through his binoculars, Captain Singh could see that the tiny vessel was burning away fast. Perhaps it was not even a vessel maybe just a dinghy or a lifeboat. The Captain knew fires don't start by themselves, not in the middle of the sea. He thought someone is onboard and they have little time left, the fire will soon consume the whole craft, he hoped they were good swimmers.

Ahead, the speedboat was closing the gap. As they got close enough, they launched a flare. The burning lightbulb curved downwards, washing the night in red light.

The Captain could see the remnants of a life raft with its sole survivor. It was a sight he would never forget. A skeleton of a man was clutching a burning piece of a paddle in his hands, even as it was burning his arms.

The life raft disintegrated below his feet, and the skeleton fell into the ocean. But somehow, with the sheer force of will, he managed to keep the burning log above the surface of water. Even as his head bobbed up and down, and he was gulping water, the burning log stayed up in his arms.

The speedboat reached him, by now, all signs of the raft had withered away in the fire. The rescue team got close to him and tried to haul him out of the water. But the skeleton man was strangely resisting them. He was pointing the burning log in their direction.

The Captain wondered, *why is he trying to keep his rescuers away?*

A soldier reached into the water and tried to grab the skeleton man's arm. Again the skeleton man screamed, "Take this first! Save her!!"

The man was clearly delirious.

The soldier realised that the only way to save him was to take that log from him first, so he reached out and grabbed the flaming log from his hand. The skeleton man handed it readily enough, and seemed relieved, till he saw the troop toss away the burning log away from them into the sea.

The skeleton man gave out a blood numbing scream.

Captain Singh felt the anguish behind the scream as he was seeing this bizarre scene unfold before him. Behind the skeleton man, all remnants of his raft had disappeared, the fire had consumed it all, and burnt out.

The log that the soldier had carelessly tossed was now bobbing on the surface of the water, still flaming, still a few embers left on the side that faced the sky.

Surprising the troops and the Captain alike, the skeleton man dived away from his rescuers and towards the burning log. The troops were baffled, but they only hesitated for a second and jumped in the water after him.

The skeleton man made a grab for the flaming log. But before he could reach it, the troops grabbed the skeleton man. He tried to pull away again, with a power that surprised the troops, but they kept their grip strong.

Then, a wave washed over the log and the embers went out.

The skeleton screamed in agony, "No!!!"

The last flame disappeared, the fire died and the waves carried the charred log away, ever so softly, into the great oblivion.

The skeleton man's struggle ended and his body grew limp. The troops hauled him on to the speedboat and headed back towards INS Vikrant. They would recall this as the strangest rescue of their life.

As they climbed back on their ship, Captain Singh asked, "No other survivors?"

"No Captain. Just him."

The skeleton man was wailing, "you killed her... you killed her...!"

The Captain looked at his troops and said, "You sure there was no one else?"

"Positive sir, we circled the area three times to be sure. Nothing on the thermal cameras too, except this guy and the fire."

Captain Singh nodded and looked at the skeleton strapped to a stretcher with a compassion that betrayed his rank. The skeleton's skin was sunburnt, muscles atrophied, hair long and dishevelled, stomach arched inwards, eyes hollow, ribs ready to break skin and arms badly burnt. He said, "Take him to the infirmary, now."

As they hauled him away, Captain Singh thought, it's a miracle this man is alive, he must have friends in high places.

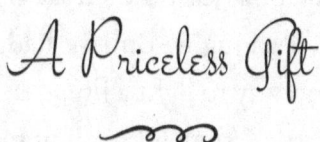

A Priceless Gift

It was the tiny Fireball who spotted the ship sailing far on the horizon. I was far too weak to even stand up and wave to it, forget rowing or signalling to it. I thought it was a cruel joke by the universe, to give us a glimmer of hope as I was at death's door.

The moon was barely a crescent and there were hardly any stars around. We didn't have a clock on us, but I guessed it was close to midnight.

There was no way a ship on the horizon, so far from us, would see us. To them we would appear as a small dot, perhaps slightly darker than the darkness that surrounded it, but invisible nonetheless.

I had saved a small piece of polished tin to use as a reflector during day, but at night we had no way left to signal for help.

Those flares I had set off on the night of my epic party

would have saved our lives tonight. They were gone now and in a not too distant future, I would be too.

The tiny Fireball said, "We can light a fire. They will be able to see the fire, or at least the smoke rising from it."

Good point, I thought. But we had nothing to burn on our raft and no way to light a fire.

"That's not true," she said reading my thoughts again. "We can set the raft itself on fire."

"I am dying anyway, so burn the raft for all I care, but how will we start the fire?"

"*I* can start a fire, I am literally a spark, in case you haven't noticed," she smiled.

"No!" I was horrified. "Then you will merge with the fire... in case you haven't noticed, my dear, we are surrounded by water, the fire will burn out soon enough, and with it, so will you. That's not an option."

She saw the ship passing on the horizon. Soon, it was going to be beyond reach.

She closed her eyes and thought of everywhere she had been, and everything she had learned on her star quest. A flood of knowledge and wisdom came back to her in that one moment.

All Life is One Life.
   We get what we give.
   The Higher Ones are ever ready to help us.
   We must live for love.
   You'll only gather timber on your star quest,

the fire will be lit by something within you,
that's greater than you.
Let your Light shine.

The tiny Fireball felt a great joy rising within her.
She lit the fire.
"Nooo...!" I screamed, as I saw her become one with the fire. I begged, I pleaded, "You can't do this! I don't want to lose you!! I don't deserve this. Think of your Moth..."

As the fire engulfed my raft, she smiled kindly and said, "I am thinking of my Moth, just as I am thinking of you. I now understand, we only live when we live for our fellow travellers. By saving you, my Moth will be saved... somehow. I might not be there with either of you, but its okay. To Save One Life is to Save All Life."

I lost all my words, no one had given me so much, sacrificed so much for me, ever.

The fire reached the bottom of the raft. The water gobbled it away like a hungry monster.

Part by part, the fire started sizzling away, and I felt a sharp physical pain, the same physical pain that the tiny Fireball was doing her best to hide from me.

She was giving up her life, her love for me.

How would I ever repay her?

She read my mind one last time, smiled her sweetest smile, the one usually reserved for her Moth, and said, "You'll find a way."

A flare went up in the air, everything turned red, help

was coming. I grabbed a blazing piece of paddle, the fire had reduced it to a mere log, still I held on to it for dear life. My flesh was burning beneath it, but it didn't matter. The tiny Fireball had become this fire, if I could save a little bit of this fire, just a tiny spark, I could save her.

The raft gave up below my feet. I fell in the water but with a sheer strength of spirit, I managed to kick my feet and keep the burning log overhead. The fire was shooting nails through the bones of my arms, but I promised myself I will not let go of of the log.

The speedboat arrived, I told them to take the log from my hand, to save my best friend first,

but...

∼

The tiny Fireball was gone.
Forever, and for good.

After I grieved and moaned and wailed; after my tears ran dry over the next few days, I figured out a way of repaying the tiny Fireball for her sacrifice.

I had to earn the gift she had given me.

Moth?

Over the years, my arms have healed completely, I experience no physical pain, but I will carry these burn marks forever.

I don't regret them, they are the memories of my sweetest friend. A careful observer will discover beautiful, matching patterns on my burnt forearms, the kind you would find on a moth's wings.

I had once joked and asked the tiny Fireball if she was my moth.

She wasn't, but maybe I was her moth all along.

I was naive, lost and had a death wish.

She saved my life, so we could say that she succeeded in her star quest, even if it cost her the ultimate sacrifice.

Maybe.

We get to choose what we believe.

It hurts me more because she was so close to her goal.

We just had to figure out how to get her into outer space. Once in space, she could easily travel back to her home star.

Escaping gravity, without any obvious fuel source was the problem. We were just one step away.

Ah well, life unfolds in mysterious ways.

I keep meditating on everything she taught me and I have reached this realisation — *Love is the eternal force that drives this Universe.*

Looking back, I can see there was an abundance of love on our little life raft.

Anyway, I must carry on now.

The kids will be home soon, and we plan to bake a surprise for their mom, she is going to love it.

I want to leave you with a little parting gift though. A question to ponder over when you have a moment or two.

If we assume I was the moth, who do you think was the tiny Fireball?

Epilogue

Captain Singh's final log entry on the incident:

The subject is making a good recovery. He is not speaking much, so identification is still not confirmed.

As per the Doctor's reports, the subject seems to have spent between 11 to 14 months stranded on a small raft. He was in a state of delirium, insisting that my team killed his friend during the rescue mission.

I have thoroughly analysed the attached video footage, thermal scans and the rescue team's body-cam footage, and I can confirm that there was no other known life form onboard his craft.

This matter is now closed.

PS: I must add, it was an unusual fire. For such a small fire with no obvious fuel source, it burned much brighter than normal. Given the distance, we would have missed it for sure if it wasn't so bright.

I noticed another unusual thing that night as we got closer to the life raft.

The fire seemed to rage higher and upwards.

It was so high, it felt like the tiny sparks at the top of the fire had reached the heavens above.

Dear reader, I hope you enjoyed this little star-hopping adventure. If this book inspires you to meditate, I'll call it a success. Meditation came into my life 19 years ago and brought light to my life. There are 3 practices I follow, the Silva method, Brahmavidya (aka Mentalphysics) and Vipassana, and I recommend them all. Check them out if you feel inspired. There are many roads up the Highest mountain, and it's not important which path we choose, but that we keep going, that we keep rising higher and higher, just like our sweetest friend, the tiny Fireball.

Love,
    Sameer Kochure.

PS: I've included information about my other books on the following pages. You can read them next if you like. I suspect there's another, yet untold, adventure hiding in the tiny Fireball's universe. If you would like to read it someday, just let me know on my website or social channels. If enough readers would like to read it, I'll start writing it. Thanks. :)

A YOUNG BOY
and his best friend,
THE UNIVERSE

Welcome to a spiritual fable that will win your heart.

See the world through the eyes of a young boy that are full of wonder and innocence.

The young boy sees what others don't and questions what the grownups won't. And boy, does he have questions. A pocket full of them.

Luckily for him, he has an equally playful friend, the Universe, by his side. The Universe helps him make sense of the world. The young boy's best friend, the Universe knows everything and helps him through life's mysteries, like a true friend.

Fall in love with these two unique characters as they laugh, cry and play together.

Discover a friendship that will leave you longing for a similar friendship in your own life. And don't be too surprised if you find yourself in the young boy's shoes once too often.

That's when you'll be the closest to your new best friend.

Part of Sameer Kochure's 'The Good Universe Series' - these books can be read and enjoyed in any order.

Welcome to a poetry collection that celebrates the strength behind the beauty that is a woman.

Inspired by stories of real women, **this collection of 100 poems honours the raw grit and the moral fortitude that exists in all women.** Sometimes that power is inherent, sometimes it needs to be invoked, but it is always there.

Page after page, you'll discover a newfound love and respect for yourself, and for all the women in your life.

Written by Sameer Kochure, the author of the much adored book series *'A Young Boy and His Best Friend, The Universe,'* and *'Wrong. - An inspirational poetry collection,'* this is an easy to read, yet strikingly powerful work of art.

This is NOT a regular book of poems on love, heartbreak or feminism. **It's a salute to the moral strength it takes to be a woman** in today's world. The steel beneath the flowers.

An empowering and a comfort read for all the thinking, feeling women around the world, and for everyone who loves them.

100 Poems | 1 Unmissable Collection

More Goodies For You

Spotify playlist: Ever wondered - *'If this book was a song what would it sound like?'* Wonder no more. Go to https://spoti.fi/3Qtwb94 or scan the QR code below and enjoy author curated Spotify playlist that perfectly compliments the book - The Tiny Fireball.

Check out **AI created art** for the this book at: **www.ChannelingHigherWisdom.com**

The eight Noble stars from this book actually represent an ancient spiritual path dating back thousands of years. Get the author's special report and learn more about it at: **www.ChannelingHigherWisdom.com**

Acknowledgments

The following names belong on the cover, for this book owes its existence to the ones who make my universe.

My family, Dr Monica, Dr Narahari and Hriday Talur. Viju maushi, Tayade uncle, Pinks, Sam, Gau, Ishaan and Khrisha. Jośe Silva, Dr Bimol Rakshit, Burt Goldman and Hemil Shah. Ding Le Mei, SN Goenkaji and Gautama, the Buddha. Hemant Moghe, Mandeep Anand and Vinay Rathod. Tejal Mamaniya, Mehboob Peerbhai and all kind souls who have lit my path.

I give thanks, I give thanks, I give thanks.

Also by Sameer Kochure

The Good Universe Series:

A Young Boy and His Best Friend, The Universe Vol. I

A Young Boy and His Best Friend, The Universe, Vol. II

A Young Boy and His Best Friend, The Universe, Vol. III

A Young Boy and His Best Friend, The Universe, Vol. VII

A Young Boy and His Best Friend, The Universe. Boxset: Books 1-3

The 1 Verse Poetry Collection:

Made of Flowers and Steel

Wrong - An Inspirational Poetry Collection

By the time you are reading this, I may have new books out. The most up to date list of my books is available at:

www.ChannelingHigherWisdom.com

An Appeal

I can live for two months on a good compliment. - Mark Twain.

If you enjoyed this book, be a rockstar and leave me a quick review, won't you? Just 1 or 2 sentences from you may help other readers discover my books. I honestly don't know if reviews help sell more books, but I know for a fact that your reviews compel me to keep writing new books. So if you enjoyed reading my words, please send me some of yours.

Wrong. An Inspirational Poetry Collection

Get your FREE copy at:
www.ChannelingHigherWisdom.com

NASA's Voyager 1 has captured a strange, rhythmic, humming sound vibrating in interstellar space.

Could it be the Universe speaking to us in poetry?

Thus begins this powerful inspirational poetry collection by Sameer Kochure, author of the much adored book series 'A Young Boy And His Best Friend, The Universe.'

Just like that beloved spiritual fable, **this book is full of wisdom shorts that'll help you live a more wholesome life.**

It takes **the inner eye, a thinking heart and a feeling mind**, to appreciate all the beauty that surrounds us. There's just so much of it out there, and the loving Universe that it is; it feeds it to us in small, right-sized portions, the ones we can truly love and appreciate.

No wonder, we keep coming back for more.

∽

Get your FREE copy at:
www.ChannelingHigherWisdom.com

About the Author

Author photo by Ahsan Ali

Sameer Kochure was born in India during the darkest part of the night. Probably explains why he is such a self-proclaimed dreamer. He has lived in 6 cities and 3 countries since. He has also clocked in 12 years as a Creative Director in some of the biggest advertising agencies across Asia Pacific. He lives in Dubai, but claims that anywhere he travels, he feels he is home.

You can follow Sameer on the following social channels and join his VIP mailing list at:
www.ChannelingHigherWisdom.com

Buy or Borrow

Libraries played a big part in nurturing my love for reading while growing up. So, to give back some of the love libraries have shown me, I have made sure that all my books are easily accessible to major libraries across the world. In case, you don't find any of my books that you want at your library, just fill out a simple book request form, all libraries have them, and more often than not, they will be happy to procure my books for you and honour your request. They love supporting loyal readers like you. Libraries are awesome that way. Show them some love as well. :)

Gratitude

Thank you for reading.
    Thank you for spreading the light.
    Thank you for keeping the fire burning.

www.ingramcontent.com/pod-product-compliance
Lightning Source LLC
LaVergne TN
LVHW030322070526
838199LV00069B/6525